A Cowboy's KISS

COWBOYS
of Crested Butte

BOOK THREE

USA TODAY BESTSELLING AUTHOR

HEATHER SLADE

A COWBOY'S KISS
© 2017 Heather Slade

This book is a work of fiction. The names, characters, places and incidents are products of the writer's imagination or have been used fictitiously and are not to be construed as real. Any resemblance to persons, living or dead, actual events, locale or organizations is entirely coincidental.

979-8-88649-101-2

Find her,
Protect her,
Spoil her,
Dance with her
And never stop
Loving her
Or someone
Else will.

MORE FROM AUTHOR HEATHER SLADE

BUTLER RANCH
Kade's Worth
Brodie's Promise
Maddox's Truce
Naughton's Secret
Mercer's Vow
Kade's Return
Butler Ranch Christmas

WICKED WINEMAKERS
FIRST LABEL
Brix's Bid
Ridge's Release
Press' Passion
Zin's Sins
Tryst's Temptation

WICKED WINEMAKERS
SECOND LABEL
Beau's Beloved
Coming Soon:
Cru's Crush
Bones' Bliss
Snapper's Seduction
Kick's Kiss

ROARING FORK RANCH
Coming Soon:
Roaring Fork Wrangler
Roaring Fork Roughstock
Roaring Fork Rockstar
Roaring Fork Rooker
Roaring Fork Bridger

THE ROYAL AGENTS
OF MI6
Make Me Shiver
Drive Me Wilder
Feel My Pinch
Chase My Shadow
Find My Angel

K19 SECURITY
SOLUTIONS TEAM ONE
Razor's Edge
Gunner's Redemption
Mistletoe's Magic
Mantis' Desire
Dutch's Salvation

K19 SECURITY
SOLUTIONS TEAM TWO
Striker's Choice
Monk's Fire
Halo's Oath
Tackle's Honor
Onyx's Awakening

K19 SHADOW OPERATIONS
TEAM ONE
Code Name: Ranger
Code Name: Diesel
Code Name: Wasp
Code Name: Cowboy
Code Name: Mayhem

K19 ALLIED INTELLIGENCE
TEAM ONE
Code Name: Ares
Code Name: Cayman
Code Name: Poseidon
Code Name: Zeppelin
Code Name: Magnet

K19 ALLIED INTELLIGENCE
TEAM TWO
Coming Soon:
Code Name: Puck
Code Name: Michelangelo
Code Name: Typhon
Code Name: Hornet
Code Name: Reaper

PROTECTORS
UNDERCOVER
Undercover Agent
Undercover Emissary
Coming Soon:
Undercover Savior
Undercover Infidel
Undercover Assassin

THE INVINCIBLES
TEAM ONE
Decked
Edged
Grinded
Riled
Smoked

THE INVINCIBLES
TEAM TWO
Bucked
Irished
Sainted
Hammered
Ripped

THE UNSTOPPABLES
TEAM ONE
Furied
Merried

COWBOYS OF
CRESTED BUTTE
A Cowboy Falls
A Cowboy's Dance
A Cowboy's Kiss
A Cowboy Stays
A Cowboy Wins

For the cowboys and cowgirls
who are brave enough
to chase their dreams.

TABLE OF CONTENTS

1

Jace Rice was tired of being the nice guy—what in the hell was wrong with him anyway? He'd fallen in love, and instead of fighting for the woman who'd captured his heart, he'd handed her over to another man. And worse? He was about to spend Thanksgiving with her.

Today he'd see Irene Fairchild for the first time since he decided to be noble instead of smart. Later, he and Tucker, his twin, would drive over the pass from Aspen to Crested Butte to spend the holiday with their cousin Ben and his family, which included Ben's stepdaughter, Irene.

The day he'd met her, he was on his way to the barns at Black Mountain Ranch, hoping to go for a long, quiet ride. Guests would begin arriving at the dude ranch the following week, and employees would no longer have time for afternoon pleasure rides.

When a car came barreling down the dirt road, his first inclination was to tell the driver to slow down, but when it came to a stop and he saw the woman driving, he'd changed his mind.

"What's your name, cowgirl?" he'd asked when she opened the door and stepped out. He'd tipped his hat, welcomed her to the ranch, and offered to help carry her bags to her cabin.

When she'd told him the number of the cabin she'd been assigned, he'd been as surprised to hear it was one of the few single cabins, as he was by his reaction. If anyone had asked, Jace would've said he had no interest in a summer romance with someone he worked with, but knowing Irene would be sleeping in her cabin alone sent his mind racing with thoughts of the two of them together.

Something about her got under his skin the moment he met her. She was beautiful, but there was more to it. Her blue eyes sparkled in the sun, and she had an easy laugh, but something or someone had hurt her, and even then, Jace vowed not to let anything hurt her again.

"Thinking about her isn't going to help." Tucker nudged him.

"What are you talking about?"

"You're thinking about her. It's over. Move on."

"Not that easy."

"It is that easy. Quit dwelling on it."

"Wait until you meet her. You'll understand."

"I don't need to meet her to understand she's engaged to another man. What else is there?"

"You'll see."

***

Blythe Cochran hadn't wanted to spend Thanksgiving in Crested Butte, but since her parents told her they were going with or without her, she gave in, hoping it wouldn't be as bad as she was afraid it would be. Instead, it was worse.

She'd hoped that things between her and her best friend since kindergarten, Renie Fairchild, would go back to the way they had always been, but after not seeing her for almost a year, it felt more like Blythe didn't know her friend anymore. Now that she was engaged, all Renie cared about was Billy, her fiancé, and his daughter, Willow.

They'd spent the morning having breakfast and shopping, and now, were headed back to the ranch. Once they got there, Blythe figured Renie would ditch her again.

When they walked in, Liv, Renie's mom, was sitting at the dining room table, feet up on a chair, with a pillow under them.

"Is everything okay?" Renie asked her.

Liv laughed. "They're babying me. Because they've forgotten I've already had one," she shouted in the direction of the kitchen.

"What is she talking about?" asked Blythe.

"My mom is having a baby."

She was? Was that even possible? God, she hoped her mom didn't decide to have another baby too.

"Blythe, be nice," Renie told her before she even said anything.

"But—"

Renie put her hand over Blythe's mouth. "I'll work on telling you how I'm feeling. You need to work on the opposite. We don't always want to hear what you're thinking, Blythe."

"Bravo!" There were claps and cheers from her mom and Liv.

"'Bout time you stood up for something, Renie," said her mom. "I'll enjoy finding out how you feel about things."

Renie rolled her eyes. "It hasn't been that bad."

"Don't pout, sweetheart," her mother said when Renie left the room to talk to Billy.

"Seriously? You're siding with Renie on this?"

"She's right," her mom said quietly. "We don't always want to hear what you're thinking. Just because your dad gets away with it doesn't mean it's okay, or that you should do the same."

Blythe was fuming. First Renie lectured her, and now her mom was adding to it. Blythe hadn't been in Crested Butte twenty-four hours, but she already wanted to go home.

"Maybe I should leave. Would that make everyone happy?"

Liv walked over and hugged her. "No, it wouldn't make everyone happy, least of all me. I'm sorry, Blythe. We're encouraging Renie to be less of a doormat, but it shouldn't be at your expense."

"What time is dinner?" Renie asked, coming back into the kitchen. "I'm thinking about going for a ride. Blythe, are you up for it?"

"I will be if you let me ride Pooh."

"Of course I will."

Blythe wasn't as comfortable around horses as Renie. In fact, they usually scared her, but Pooh was different. She was easy and gentle.

"Which horse are you riding?" Blythe asked while they put on their jackets and boots.

"Micah needs some exercise. I'll take him."

Micah was the horse Liv rode as a competitive barrel racer, something she'd taken up last year. Blythe thought she was crazy and said so after Liv was badly injured but started competing again soon after she'd recovered.

"Liv would be miserable if she'd quit," her mother had explained at the time. "It's been her lifelong dream to compete."

Blythe understood what that meant on a philosophical level, but there wasn't anything she'd personally felt strongly enough about to call a dream. She'd been in nursing school, but quit, saying she hadn't liked it as much as she expected. Truthfully, she hated it.

"I'm thinking about going back to school," Renie told her on their way to the barn.

Right around the same time Blythe quit the nursing program, Renie transferred from Dartmouth, where she was studying biomedicine, to the Colorado State University in Fort Collins. She'd planned to become a large animal vet but had dropped out of that program too last year.

"When?"

"After Billy and I get married."

Renie and Billy were getting married. It would take some time for that to sink in. Especially since Billy, eleven years older than they were, discovered he had a daughter he hadn't known about, and the baby's mother had passed away.

Renie broke up with Billy over it, and for a long while, Blythe didn't think they'd ever speak again. Not that Blythe had heard any of this first hand.

"It's so pretty here, don't you think?" Renie asked, motioning toward the wide-open vistas of the ranch.

Blythe nodded. It was a beautiful day. The sun was shining, the sky was blue, and maybe, if she got lucky, she'd meet one of the many cowboys who worked the Flying R Ranch when they rode out.

They were almost inside the barn when someone drove up in a truck and honked the horn. It came to a stop, and Blythe watched as two crazily good-looking men climb out of it.

"Hey, there," one of them shouted to Renie.

"*Who. Is. That?*" Blythe asked.

"Jace and his brother. I'll introduce you," she said over her shoulder.

"There are two of them? Oh, my God, I've died and gone to heaven."

One of the two men raced over, picked Renie up, and swung her around in a circle. The other frowned.

"Who's this?" the sullen one asked.

"This is Irene," the other said. "Irene, meet Tucker. And this is...I don't know who this is."

"This is Blythe," answered Renie. "Her mom and my mom are best friends. We are, too. Have been since we were five years old. Blythe, this is Jace Rice."

Blythe hoped her palms weren't as sweaty as she was afraid they were when Jace shook her hand and held on a little longer than necessary. "It's a pleasure to meet you," he said softly, making her blush.

"I'm Tucker," said his twin, who walked forward and took her hand in his. She couldn't explain the tremor she felt at his touch, or the heat that spread throughout her body when she met his penetrating gaze.

Renie cleared her throat. "We were headed out for a ride."

"We'll let you be on your way, then." Tucker slowly let go of Blythe's hand, breaking the spell he had her under.

When she turned around to follow Renie back to the barn, she caught a glimpse of the scowl Jace was leveling at his brother.

When he saw she was watching, Jace smiled at her. "I'll look forward to seeing you when you get back."

"Likewise," she answered but then looked at Tucker. "I guess I'll see you too."

Tucker didn't respond, but the smoldering look he gave her said everything.

"Are you ready?" Renie snapped, startling her with both the tone she used and the daggers she shot in her direction.

What had she done wrong now? This nonsense was quickly getting old. Once they were out on the trail, Blythe intended to give Renie a piece of her mind. Just because Renie had decided to alter her personality did not mean she had *carte blanche* to suggest Blythe do the same.

"What the hell is your problem?" Blythe said when they were far enough away from the barn that no one could hear them.

Renie shrugged.

"Seriously? That's it? What happened to your promise to be more forthright with how you feel about things?"

"That's Jace," she murmured.

"Yes, I know. You introduced me to him."

"I spent the summer with Jace while Billy and I were apart."

Interesting. So, was his flirtation only intended to make Renie jealous? *"Well, all-righty then.* Scratch another one off the eligible-bachelor list. How about Tucker? You haven't had a fling with him too, have you?"

Renie rolled her eyes. "No, Blythe. I haven't."

"Maybe it would be easier for both of us if you gave me a list of the men you'd like me to stay away from."

"It isn't like that."

"Billy is hands off, now Jace is too."

"That's it. Those two make up my entire list of male conquests." Renie laughed, and when she did, Blythe was relieved. She had begun to doubt Renie still possessed a sense of humor.

"So, tell me," Blythe said, changing the subject. "How is it being the wicked stepmother?"

"Are you really interested, or is it a show to get back at the ex-girlfriend?" Tucker asked his brother.

"Her name is Irene. And yes, I'm interested."

"You're sure?"

"Did you see her? She's magnificent."

Tucker agreed. She was magnificent. Her violet-hued eyes had sparkled when she met his gaze, stirring something in him that he hadn't felt in a long while. He'd almost reached forward to run his fingers through her silky dark hair.

"Can't you feel it?" Tucker asked, but his brother turned away without answering.

Sometimes he wondered if he could feel Jace more than his twin could feel him. Even if they were a thousand miles apart, Tucker felt his twin's turmoil.

Tucker hadn't wanted to spend Thanksgiving in Crested Butte, but Jace insisted. When their parents agreed and his father told him how much he was looking forward to reconnecting with his cousin, Tucker succumbed.

"We were close once," his father had said. "But we drifted apart after your grandfather died. We used to come to Crested Butte for Thanksgiving every year, but when you boys were born, I knew it would be easier on your mom if we stayed home."

His father's words were the only reason Tucker had agreed to come along on a day he normally kept to himself.

Until last week, Tucker had been in Spain, where he spent as much time as he could. Since he'd gotten back to the States, he'd been adrift. At first he thought it was jet lag, but when he wasn't feeling better after a week, he knew the only thing that would assuage his angst, was letting the artist in him get back to work.

Most recently he'd completed several sculptures done in bronze. He'd sold them all, even the one he'd intended to keep for himself. He considered block prints next, but painting was beckoning him.

It had been three years since he'd painted. Watercolor was his favorite medium in two-dimensional work. He could paint quickly—a sense of accomplishment came immediately. There were days he could do three or four full-sheet paintings before noon. He longed for that kind of release.

There was more to his bad mood than lack of a project, though. He was beginning to feel as though his life was aimless. When he was younger he'd believed he'd have love, a family, everything his parents had, but that dream had died, only to come alive again today, when something in Blythe's dark-haired beauty spoke to him.

If he pursued her, would his interest in her last? Or, as it had with so many other women, would he tire of her quickly? There'd only been one woman in his life who'd been able to hold his attention. When he lost her, he lost hope that anyone ever would again.

"I'm attracted to her," he finally said.

"I know," Jace answered.

"So you felt it."

"I was ignoring you."

"What should we do?" Tucker asked.

"Let her choose."

"This could get ugly, Jace."

"Maybe she won't choose either of us."

Tucker shook his head and laughed. "Right."

It wouldn't be the first time he and his brother vied for a woman's affections, both knowing it was more about the thrill of the chase than the catch. This time, though, Tucker doubted Jace had any idea that, to him, it wasn't a game.

2

"This place is spectacular." Blythe looked out at the scenery surrounding them. "I thought your mom's place was beautiful. This is…I don't know…almost too much for words."

"It is, isn't it?"

Looking north through meadows full of tall grasses, the southern face of Mount Crested Butte was visible. A river ran through the center of the valley; cattle roamed the south side of the river, and horses were kept to the north. Blythe couldn't imagine how beautiful it must be in winter, when snow covered the ground and the surrounding mountains. Or in the spring, when the ranch was blanketed in the spectacular wild flowers Crested Butte was known for.

Now, though, in the fall when the Aspens showed their golden splendor that mixed with the reds and oranges of the other deciduous trees, all against the backdrop of the deep blue Colorado sky, Blythe couldn't imagine there was a more beautiful place on earth.

"Tell me what you know about the twins," Blythe said once they were farther out on the trail.

"I don't know much about Tucker. He's an artist. They share a condo in Aspen, and it's full of his work."

"What kind of art?"

"Everything, from what I saw. He's a painter, but a sculptor, too. Jace said he gets bored with one medium and moves on to another."

"How did he get the scar?" She probed knowing she probably shouldn't.

"Scar? I have no idea. I didn't notice, to be honest."

"He seems broody."

"Then you're perfectly suited to one another."

"Very funny. Jace seemed more interested than the broody one anyway."

"Jace is a really good guy." Renie looked off in the distance.

"Regretting your choice? I'd be happy to reconsider Billy Patterson if you're thinking of letting him go. Although…"

"What?"

"The baby."

"Don't give it too much thought, Blythe. There is no way I'm ever letting go of Billy Patterson. He's mine, and I'm keeping him."

Blythe had been hot for Billy for a long time, but admittedly, she didn't know him very well, not the way Renie did.

"I'm happy for you, Renie."

"Thank you, Blythe. I know that wasn't easy for you to admit."

"So, what should we do tonight?"

"I know what I'll be doing, and I'm sure it won't interest you."

"What's that?"

"I'll be at home, with my future husband and our baby."

"Ugh. You're right. Doesn't interest me at all. Why did you invite me if you don't plan to spend any time with me?"

"I haven't left your side since you got here. I'll be with you all day tomorrow, too."

"So you're saying I'm on my own tonight."

"Poor Blythe. Whatever will you do?"

"I was hoping to stumble on a cowboy or two out on our ride. Where are they anyway? Isn't this a ranch?"

Renie laughed but didn't answer.

Blythe was relieved when Renie turned Micah around and rode back toward the house. She probably could've ridden for another hour, but Blythe always lost interest in it before her friend did.

She wondered how Renie would react if Jace ended up being as interested as he'd acted when they met. Would she tell Blythe he was off limits? It didn't really matter. Blythe was far more interested in Tucker anyway. There was something about him that intrigued her. It wasn't his looks; they were identical twins. It was more, but she couldn't put her finger on what it was that drew her to him.

Ben Rice and Billy Patterson were sitting at the dining room table, talking to Jace and Tucker when they came back in the house. Liv, Paige, and Mark were in the kitchen, nearby.

"Where's Willow?" Renie asked, bending down to kiss Billy's cheek.

"Downstairs, with Ben's boys," he answered, turning to kiss her lips.

Renie raised an eyebrow.

"It's okay," he said. "We have to let her go sometime. She'll be fine. Jake and Luke are great with her."

"Can't we wait until she's at least in the double digits before we cast her off into the world alone?"

"You're so maternal," Jace said.

"She is, isn't she?" Billy sounded proud.

"Does that surprise you?" Blythe asked.

"Not at all, actually." Jace turned so he was facing her directly. "How 'bout you, Blythe? Are you maternal?"

"Uh, no," she laughed. "Billy picked the right girl, no question. Renie will love Willow to pieces."

"You wouldn't love her?" When Tucker spoke, everyone at the table turned and looked at him.

Blythe's face turned red. "I didn't say I wouldn't love her. I said I'm not as maternal as Renie is." She stood and went into the kitchen, not that the rooms had much separation, and put her arms around her father's waist.

"What's wrong, sweetie?" he asked.

She pointed in the direction of the table. "He was mean to me, Daddy." Everyone knew she was being silly, which took the heat off the embarrassment she felt at Tucker's words.

"Who was? Let's see who I can get to beat him up for you. Any takers, or will I have to send Paige after him?"

Her mom slugged him.

"See? She can take all of you, even the mean one."

The guys at the table were still looking at Tucker.

"What?" he finally asked.

"You should apologize," Jace answered.

"For what?"

"You're making this too easy for me," he muttered.

Tucker got up and went into the kitchen. "I'm sorry I offended you. Although I'm still not sure what I said wrong."

"Nice apology, man," laughed Mark. "I'm sorry, but I don't know why."

"Come on," Tucker said to Blythe. "Go for a walk with me."

"Why?"

"So you can get even with me for hurting your feelings."

"Shouldn't I refuse to go for a walk with you? Wouldn't that hurt your feelings?"

"I bet you can do a whole lot better than that given the extra time."

Tucker held her jacket for her, and she followed when he walked out the front door.

She studied him from behind. He had strong shoulders and a tight little butt, powerful thighs, and those arms. How much time did he spend at the gym? She hoped not too much; she couldn't stand guys who talked about working out all the time.

When he got to the bottom of the porch steps, he stopped, turned around, and circled her waist with the arms she'd just been drooling over. He startled her, but having him that close—wow. His green eyes were piercing, and she wanted to run her fingers through his long, sandy-blond hair. The scar on the left side of Tucker's face made it easy to tell the two brothers apart. That and their hair. Jace kept his cropped short; Tucker's was long.

"I'm sorry," he whispered as his hand came up and cupped the back of her neck. "Forgive me?"

"What are you doing?" she laughed. She put her hands on his chest as if to push him away but got lost in the feel of his rock-hard pecs.

His arm tightened around her waist, and he pulled her into him. "Apologizing," he answered.

"This is an apology? You're a little *gropy* with your 'I'm sorries,' aren't you?"

"Can't help myself."

At first she thought he'd kiss her, but instead, he rested his cheek against hers. "You're magnificent," he murmured.

"What's goin' on out here?" Jace asked, coming out the front door.

Blythe tried to wriggle free from Tucker's hold, but he tightened it instead.

"I'm apologizing," Tucker answered.

"Looks like you've got my girl in a death grip," smirked Jace.

Blythe pushed at Tucker harder. "Are your arms made of steel?"

"No, that's his will." Jace laughed.

Tucker didn't answer. He didn't let go of her either. And when she looked back at him, his eyes were focused on her mouth.

"Go away," he growled at his brother.

Jace turned toward the front door. "This isn't over," Blythe heard him say before he went inside.

"What was that all about? I'm not going to be a—"

Before she could finish, Tucker kissed her. And it wasn't a chaste kiss. It was exactly the kind of kiss she'd expected from him. His hand moved from the back of her neck up to cup her head, and he plundered her mouth with his.

When his other hand came up to cup her breast, she swatted at it. "Stop that."

He did, and then she was sorry she'd told him to. He let go of her and walked away.

"Wait. Where are you going?"

"For a walk."

Just as she was about to go back in the house, he turned around. "Are you coming or not?"

She was intrigued enough to follow.

He walked toward his truck, stopped, and opened the driver's door.

"I thought you were going for a walk."

"Changed my mind. Come on, get in." He motioned to the door.

"You want me to drive?"

"No, I don't want you to drive," he mimicked her. "Get in and slide over."

Blythe wasn't sure why, but it didn't matter what Tucker told her to do, she did it without hesitation.

"Where are we going?" she asked.

"Have you eaten?"

"No."

"To dinner."

They drove the rest of the way into town in silence. Instead of stopping downtown, Tucker kept going in the direction of the ski area. He parked in the main lot and held the door open for her.

He took her hand and led her into a courtyard. As much as Blythe wanted to ask where they were going, she doubted he'd give her a straight answer. It didn't really matter anyway, she'd go wherever he led, liking the feel of his hand holding hers.

He took her into a crowded restaurant where they were greeted by a very young, very cute blonde who asked if they had reservations.

"We'll sit at the bar," Tucker answered, pulling Blythe along behind him.

"There he is," said the man behind the bar. "How the hell are you?" He came around and gave Tucker one of those man hugs where they patted each other on the back a little too hard.

"Chris, this is Blythe," Tucker introduced them. "Chris and his wife, Kate, own the place. Where is she anyway?"

"She's in the back, but I know she'll want to see you. I'll get you seated and then go get her."

"We can sit at the bar, it's fine."

"No, no. I've got a table right here for you."

The periphery of each table was draped in fabric that hung from the ceiling. It didn't make the table completely private, but it lent an air of romance.

"I like this place," Blythe said once Chris left the table.

"Me, too." He leaned toward her. "It's sexy."

She laughed. It was sexy, but it wasn't the word she expected to him to use.

"I'll order for us."

"Do I have a choice?"

That was the response he expected from her. If she had demurely agreed, he would've been disappointed. He wasn't interested in a meek response. He wouldn't care if she fought him every step of the way, challenged him, and argued with him. That's what he wanted. He saw the fire in her, he liked it, and he wanted it.

Her phone chirped, and she put her hand in her pocket. "Do you mind?"

"Go ahead," he answered. "Then turn it off and put it away. I want your undivided attention tonight."

She excused herself and went outside. He liked that she wasn't the type to answer her cell in a room full of people.

Where are you? Renie's text said.

Restaurant at the ski area. Let my mom know. Okay?

How long will you be there?

No idea. Turning cell off now. Let her know. Thanks.

Blythe stood outside a few minutes longer, composing herself before going back in.

From the moment they met, Blythe felt something different than she ever had before. Tucker's touch electrified her. He didn't just look at her, he stared into her soul, and when he held her in his arms and kissed her, she didn't want him to ever let her go.

For the first time in her life, Blythe wanted a man in a way she'd never known existed. She closed her eyes tightly and prayed he felt the same way, and that this wasn't just a game between Jace and him.

She walked over to a roaring fire in a pit in the middle of the courtyard. She'd let him wonder a few more minutes, she certainly was.

He was grinning when Chris came back to the table and sat down.

"Kate will be out shortly. She can't wait to see you." Chris leaned in closer. "How are you, Tucker?"

"Same as always. Nothing much changes with me."

They chatted for a few minutes while Tucker looked over the wine list. "Where's your date?" Chris asked when enough time had passed that, if she had gone to the ladies' room, she would be back.

"Outside. Making me wait."

"Ah. This explains the grin. It's nice to see you this way. How long have the two of you been together?"

"About an hour."

"Ah, I see. I'm going to enjoy watching the drama unfold tonight. Thank you for bringing her here."

When Kate approached the table, both men stood.

"Tucker Rice. Is it ever good to see you." She kissed him on the lips. "How was Spain? Fight any bulls, or were your escapades limited to senoritas?"

"Careful, darling," warned Chris. "His date will be back any moment."

"Tucker, I'm so pleased. A date? Someone special I hope?"

"Someone he's known for an hour."

Kate shook her head. "That's our Tucker." She pulled her husband away from the table. "Let's watch from afar."

"Before my wife banishes me from your table, may I bring you a bottle of wine?"

"The Marqués de Murrieta Rioja."

"*Outstanding.* In honor of your recent trip, or is its spiciness in honor of the lady you're out with tonight?"

"The lady, of course."

Tucker saw Blythe walking toward the table as Chris went off to fetch the wine.

"Pleasant conversation?" he asked.

"It was a text," she smiled. "I warmed myself by the fire for a few minutes."

He wrapped his arm around her shoulder and put his lips below her ear. "I will give you all the warmth you need, Blythe. Remember that."

"So...tell me about...Jace."

Oh, he liked this girl, very much. This was going to be fun.

"Why would I spend the precious time I have with you, talking about my brother?"

"Because I asked, and I'm interested."

"Interested in him? And yet, you're here with me."

"What went on between Jace and Renie?"

Tucker didn't want to talk about Jace, for obvious reasons. But more, he didn't want to talk about Jace and Irene. It wasn't his story to tell.

"I have a better idea. Why don't you tell me what went on between you and…Renie. Is that what you call her?"

"What makes you think anything went on between us?"

He liked the way her cheeks turned pink when he brought it up. She was uncomfortable, not as confident as she had been when she came in from outside.

Watching her switch back and forth was fascinating. She was haughty one minute, and then the next, unsure of herself. He longed to paint her. His fingers itched with his need.

When Chris returned to the table with their bottle of wine, Blythe breathed an audible sigh. She might think she'd gotten a reprieve, but Tucker was nowhere near finished rattling the beautiful Miss Cochran.

He watched as Chris' eyes lit up with amusement as he and Blythe chatted. His friend wasn't giving much away, but Tucker doubted he'd hesitate to share his opinion the next time they saw each other. Would Kate also be paying their table a visit soon?

"Chris and his wife are two of my closest friends," Tucker told Blythe.

"How do you know each other?"

Chris gave him a look Tucker wished he hadn't. He didn't want to spend his time with Blythe talking about the things that had happened when he was a teenager.

"Tuck and I grew up together."

"In Aspen?"

"Yes, in Aspen." Tucker couldn't help but smile when Blythe did. She'd caught the look between Chris and him and wasn't about to let it go.

"Was Jace part of your youthful antics?"

Chris laughed out loud and excused himself from their table. "It was nice meeting you, Blythe. I look forward to many amusing conversations with you in the future."

Tucker took her hand in his and brought it to his lips. "I thought we agreed not to bring Jace with us tonight."

"You know Jace," she answered. "He pushes his way in."

Again, her charm made him laugh. He turned her hand over and kissed her palm. When he opened his mouth and kissed it again, he felt her shudder.

Jace sat at the table in Ben and Liv's house, listening to the uneasy banter taking place between his cousin and Irene's fiancé. He got the impression Ben wasn't a fan of Billy's. The feeling appeared to be mutual, and Jace wondered what was behind it. He looked over at Irene, who stood in the kitchen with the baby in her arms. She nipped playfully at the baby's fingers when she tugged on her necklace.

He'd seen her interact with kids at the ranch, and she was always good with them. He wouldn't expect her to be any different with a baby than she was with them.

Jace shifted his gaze from her, back to the table and caught Billy's eye. He hadn't missed Jace's lingering look at his fiancée.

"Where'd your brother go?" Billy asked rather than call him out.

"He and Blythe went for a drive."

"Huh."

"Huh, what?"

"Nothin'."

"You have somethin' on your mind, say it."

Billy shook his head and looked toward the kitchen, where Liv and Paige stood with Irene and Willow.

"It's nothin'," he murmured. His gaze shifted back to Mark, who'd also picked up on what was transpiring.

Jace stood and went outside. Where had Tucker taken Blythe and why had they been gone so long?

If he was smart, he'd let go of this thing between the three of them before it went any further. It already felt too much like it had one other time, with another girl they were both drawn to. He'd learned the hard way then what happened when he and Tuck wanted the same woman. And at this time of year, the memories were especially strong.

Jace had felt a spark when Irene introduced him to Blythe, and thought she had, too. When he felt it, he knew this would be more than a game, she'd be more than a girl he and Tuck would woo and try to win, only to forget about once they had.

If only he could force himself to deny his attraction to her. But, like before, she had taken hold. He couldn't let go yet, even knowing what might happen.

Blythe would be on shaky ground with him and his brother. Shakier than she'd realize. She wore her insecurity on her sleeve, and Tucker would use that to his advantage. Tucker's broodiness might sweep her up, but Jace knew she'd respond to his softer side too.

Where Tucker sometimes lacked a certain gentility, Jace was a cowboy and a gentleman. Cowboys had a code when it came to women. Actually, cowboys had a code about everything, but women in particular.

Find her, protect her, spoil her, dance with her, and never stop loving her. Or someone else will.

Blythe looked like a woman who had never been treated the *cowboy way,* and he was just the man to show her how that felt. He'd let it go for tonight. He had at least two more days to woo Miss Blythe away from his brother, and he intended to make the most of it.

The other truth of it was, he needed the distraction. It hurt like hell to watch Irene embrace a life without him in it. When he came home from Spain a few weeks ago, all he could think about was seeing her. He had such plans for them. And then, in less than twenty-four hours, he realized she'd never be his. There hadn't been any point in fighting for her. It only would've prolonged the inevitable.

Again with the damn cowboy code. He chose to be honorable. He'd called Billy Patterson himself and told him how to get his girl back. Not that Patterson had needed the advice.

3

If Tucker's aim was to woo her, he'd picked the perfect place to do it. The setting was intimate and romantic. Tucker knew a lot about wine and chose the perfect red to complement the small plates the restaurant was known for.

"What are these?" Blythe asked him when the waiter brought another plate to the table. "They look like jalapeños."

"Close. They're shishito peppers, which are from the same family, but these are sweet rather than spicy, and stuffed with almonds."

A few minutes later, the waiter delivered another plate with what looked like a thin-crust pizza. "And this?" she asked.

"Catalonian flatbread."

"Renie mentioned you were recently in Spain. Do you miss it?"

"I did, until I met a fascinating and very beautiful girl in Colorado."

She blushed. "And what are these?" She pointed to something on the flatbread.

"Those are dates and caramelized onions, sprinkled with blue cheese."

It was all so good, Blythe couldn't eat another bite, until Tucker ordered blood orange sorbet. It was light enough that she could allow herself a decadent spoonful or two.

All evening he'd watched every move she made. At first she found it disconcerting, but it hadn't taken long before she began to enjoy it. No man had ever paid this kind of attention to her.

As much as she'd wanted to leave earlier, to get away from Renie's criticism, now she was glad she hadn't. Spending time with Tucker tonight made up for Renie's indifference ten-fold.

At first she was nervous, and tried to initiate conversation. When he told her he didn't want to talk about his brother, she asked about his scar.

"Not something I talk about," he'd responded, but not in a way that made her feel self-conscious for asking.

She didn't ask any more questions, and even though they didn't talk much, she found she wasn't bored or uncomfortable. Tucker seemed content to watch her, as if her every movement, even breathing, spoke to him in a way words wouldn't.

He took her hand in his and ran his fingers over her wrist bone, and then circled it, over and over. He studied her fingers and the palm of her hand.

"I want to paint your delicacy," he whispered, making her shudder.

He gently laid her hand on the table and moved her fingers so her palm was flat against the white tablecloth, with her fingers slightly bent. He moved the candle and traced the shadow her hand cast.

If he could get this lost in her hand, what would making love with him be like? When she closed her eyes and pictured them together, he lifted her hand and kissed her palm, open-mouthed, like he had before. It was as though he read her thoughts.

"We should go," she said with regret, knowing it was late, but not wanting their night to end.

"I'm not finished with you yet, Blythe."

"I'm not finished with you either," she murmured.

He held her chair, and when she stood and he grazed her cheek with his lips, she felt a tremor stronger than any she'd felt before. If she didn't get back to the ranch, and away from this man, she'd likely do something she might live to regret. After only a few short hours, Blythe was ready to hand Tucker Rice her heart. She'd be devastated if he didn't want it.

"What is this, playing?" she asked when they were a few minutes into their drive. "It sounds familiar."

The tempo of the combined trumpet and piano was audaciously slow, as if the music might drift apart at any moment.

"*Blue in Green,*" she remembered before he answered. It had been so long since she'd heard it.

"You know it."

"My father loves Miles."

"It's my favorite piece of music on this recording. The depth of feeling…" As his voice drifted off without him finishing his thought, Blythe wondered again what making love with him would be like. Would it be slow, subtle, transcending like the music? She closed her eyes and imagined their two bodies moving together.

The truck came to a stop, and she looked around, wondering why Tucker had parked near the entrance to the ranch.

"I have to do this," he said, his hand cupping the back of her neck as it had before. He brought his lips to hers and kissed her, like she imagined he would.

Heat spread throughout her body, and as much as she wanted him to, she knew he wouldn't hurry. It would never matter what they were doing; Tucker would never hurry. Spending only a few short hours with him had taught her that.

When Tucker pulled away from her and drove the rest of the way to the house, she wondered if she'd done something wrong. Had she been too eager?

"Don't," he said without her saying a word. "When you and I are together for the first time, it won't be on the bench seat of a truck."

He didn't turn to look at her when he spoke, but his tone resonated, telling her he felt the same way she did. The same need, same desire, same impatience, but this wasn't the time or the place. They both knew that too.

Blythe was surprised when they pulled up and found the house dark and quiet. Her parents were night owls, but it had been a long day, and tomorrow would be equally so.

Tucker held her hand in his as they walked through the house, and downstairs. Blythe rested her hand on the doorknob of Renie's room where she was staying, wondering if he'd follow her in. Instead, he kissed her quickly and went into the room directly across the hall, leaving her feeling both relieved and bereft.

Tucker wished he'd arranged for a place to stay in town, instead of here, in a bedroom across the hall form a woman his body pulsed with need for. He groaned, knowing sleep would not come easy for him tonight.

Jace saw it was after midnight when he looked over at the clock. He heard them come downstairs, but they didn't speak. If they had, he would've heard every word. Seconds later, he heard both doors close.

He knew nothing had happened between them, or rather he would've known if it had. He felt Tucker's pull to the girl, though. It was as strong as his own.

The mood throughout the house tonight had been joyful. His parents had arrived shortly after Tucker and Blythe left, and were disappointed they'd missed him, but the reunion between his father and Ben's had been heartwarming.

Tomorrow was Thanksgiving, and Tucker didn't do holidays, this one in particular. When his brother withdrew, like Jace knew he would, he'd have his chance to make Blythe the center of his attention. Tucker wasn't the only Rice man with charm. He had it too, and he intended to use it.

Blythe couldn't sleep. Every time she drifted off, thoughts of Tucker woke her. She wondered what tomorrow would be like for them. Would he be demonstrative affectionately, like he'd been tonight? Would he continue to woo her in front of their families, or would he pull back?

What about Jace? What had he meant when he said it wasn't over? Again, she worried that, if this turned out to be nothing more than a competition between them, she'd be devastated.

She tossed and turned most of the night, and when she heard noises coming from the kitchen, she got out of bed and went upstairs. She didn't care who else was awake. She needed someone to talk to—as long as it wasn't Jace or Tucker.

"Morning, Daddy," she said, happy he was the one she found puttering around the kitchen.

"Where'd you go last night?"

"Tucker took me out for dinner."

"Mighty unsociable of you, wasn't it?"

"I doubt anyone noticed I was gone."

"I noticed."

"I'm sure no one else did."

"Oh please, Blythe. Don't play poor-me. You're above that kind of crap. Since when do you care what anyone else thinks?"

"It was Mom and Renie. My best friend and *my* *mother*. I'm not supposed to care what they think? Come on, Dad."

"Take it in the context it was meant. Renie is a doormat. She always has been. It's time she stood up for herself, and as it relates to you...hand it right back to her. There isn't anything that says one of you needs to be the walker and the other, walked-on. You're equals."

"It's weird."

"Billy and Renie?"

"And a baby. You don't think that's weird? And Liv is pregnant. Weirdness surrounds us."

"I heard that," said Liv, joining them in the kitchen. She sat down on the bar stool next to Blythe.

"Coffee, or are you abstaining?" Mark asked.

"Give me coffee or die," she answered.

"Okay. Not abstaining."

"Did you have fun last night? Where did Tucker take you?"

"We went to a restaurant near the ski area."

"Nice." Liv wrapped her hands around the cup of coffee her dad set in front of her.

"It was very romantic."

"You were wooed," Liv smiled.

"There's more where that came from, sugar," said Jace, walking into the kitchen, too. He stopped to pour himself a cup of coffee. "My turn today."

"Your turn for what?" asked Mark.

"Wooin' your daughter. Tucker stole her away last night. I won't let him get away with it again today." Jace walked over and sat on the other side of Blythe.

"I'm not a thing for you to compete over. I'm a person. I'm not interested in participating in whatever game the two of you are playing."

"No game, darlin'. I told you yesterday I wanted to get to know you. Didn't I?"

"I don't remember."

Mark walked to the refrigerator and rummaged around for anything that looked like breakfast food.

"Want some help?" asked Liv, joining him. She lowered her voice. "Should we leave them alone?"

"Not sure that's a good idea," Mark whispered back.

"Aren't you uncomfortable?"

"Very."

"I have a few last minute items to get from the market. Will you run me into town?"

"You got it."

Liv and her dad left the room, which Blythe was not happy about.

"We're alone now," she said. "Let's lay this on the line. I meant what I said. I'm not a toy, Jace. Just because I'm the only single woman here this weekend doesn't mean you and Tucker have to win me over. It's Thanksgiving weekend, not singles' weekend."

"If you could do anything you wanted to do today, what would it be?" Jace asked, acting as though he hadn't heard a word she said.

"No idea. I haven't had enough coffee to start thinking about it."

"Let's go get somethin' a little stronger, then. Irene took me to this great place, Rumors was the name of it. They have espresso. That oughta get your motor runnin'."

"Jace, it's Thanksgiving. I'm sure they're closed."

"Oh. You're right. I bet there'd be somethin' open at the ski area."

"*That's* what I'd do."

"What?"

"Ski. You asked what I'd do if I could do anything I wanted to. That's it. I'd ski."

"Let's do it, then."

"What? Again I remind you, it's Thanksgiving."

"So? Are you on kitchen duty today?"

"No one would want my help in the kitchen," she laughed. "I'm not what you'd call a chef."

"Okay, then. Let's go skiing. Dinner isn't until later this afternoon. They don't need our help."

"Um…"

"What? Say what's on your mind, Blythe."

"What about Tucker?"

"He already knows we're spending the day together."

"He does?"

"Yep."

"He doesn't mind?"

"Not at all. He got you last night, today you're mine."

"Oh." Blythe hoped the hurt she felt wasn't obvious. So it was a game. Tucker had happily relinquished her to his brother today after making her feel like she was the most special woman on earth last night. Her fear was realized this morning and it made her sick to her stomach.

"What are you thinking about, beautiful girl?"

If Tucker didn't care, why should she? Instead of wallowing in disappointment, she'd let Jace woo her all he wanted.

"I should talk to my mom first, but if she doesn't mind, I'm all for it."

"Go talk. I'll get my stuff together. We'll leave in twenty minutes."

"Twenty minutes? Are you crazy? I can't be ready in twenty minutes. It'll take me at least an hour to get ready."

"If that's what you need, darlin', take it. While you get ready, I'll make breakfast."

Blythe expected him to give her a hard time about taking an hour to get ready, but he didn't. He was far too good-natured about it.

Instead of tracking down her mom, she went to get ready. Jace was right, no one would need her help with dinner. If anything, there'd be too many people in the kitchen. And since he hadn't pushed, she'd see if she could get ready faster and surprise him.

Thirty minutes later, Blythe came upstairs, ready to go.

"Look at you," he said, not seeming to notice the time. He walked over to the oven and pulled out two plates, which he set on the breakfast bar.

While she got ready, Jace had made omelets, sausage, and toast. There was even a fresh pot of coffee brewing.

She couldn't help herself, though. She had to ask. "You're sure Tucker won't want to join us?"

"I already told you; it's my turn today. I get you all to myself, except for the other people skiing and slidin' out on the slopes."

"Jace—"

"Blythe." He smiled. "Two people on a lift, that's the right number. Three won't fit."

"Most chairlifts hold four."

"That'd be too crowded."

"I have to rent skis. I didn't bring mine."

"Took care of it. We're picking up Irene's for you, and Billy's for me on our way to the ski area."

She finished eating and got up to take care of the dishes. Why not do this? Hadn't she told Renie she wanted her to fix her up with a hot cowboy, or a skier? Jace was both. Made to order. She wouldn't give Tucker another thought, since he wasn't giving any to her.

Her only worry was that they had to pick up the skis, which meant she'd have to see Renie. Yesterday, she'd warned her away from Jace. She wasn't going to be happy about the two of them going skiing today. And with her new non-doormat policy, she'd probably confront Blythe about it.

"Ready?"

"Maybe this isn't such a good idea."

"Wait, what happened? You were all in a few minutes ago."

"To tell you the truth, Renie told me you were off limits yesterday."

Jace's demeanor changed. His body tensed. He walked over and took her hand. "Let's go," he said, his voice no longer playful.

"I'm sorry."

"You have nothing to be sorry for and neither do I. From where I sit, *Renie* is engaged to Billy. She doesn't dictate who you or I spend time with. It's none of her business."

When they got to Billy's, he asked whether she'd prefer to wait in the truck.

"I'm not hiding from her, Jace. We just haven't been very close lately, and I don't want to make it worse."

"Come on, then."

Renie glared at her when they came in the back door, and Jace noticed right away.

He walked over and stood right in front of her. "Knock it off," he said. "Not your business."

Renie looked stunned. Blythe didn't know Jace very well, but from what she'd seen so far, this behavior was out of character.

When he turned his back, Renie raised her eyebrows at Blythe, who burst out laughing. Which made Renie laugh. Soon the two of them were doubled over, in tears.

"What's goin' on?" Billy asked, walking into the kitchen with Willow.

"Evidently, they think I'm funny." Jace turned to the two of them, who were holding onto each other, still laughing. "Which I'm not."

"Uh huh." Blythe could hardly speak she was laughing so hard.

"They're always like this," said Billy. "They don't even have to say anything. All of a sudden they both start laughing and they can't stop. It's been that way as long as I've known 'em."

Before they came inside, Blythe told him her friendship with Renie was rocky. Maybe the best thing he could do for her today was give her a chance to spend time with someone who meant something to her.

"You wanna go with us?" Jace asked Billy. "The lifts don't open for another hour. I bet there'd be plenty of folks back at the house who'd take care of Willow."

Billy looked at Irene, who shrugged her shoulders. The look on her face was hopeful though.

"I'm not very good," said Billy. "Renie's been trying to teach me, and I've taken a few lessons, but…"

"It'll be fine, Billy. You're better than you think," Irene told him.

"As long as this isn't a competition," Billy glared at Jace.

"I'm a former racer, Billy. You don't stand a chance in hell of competing with me. I'll win before you get your skis on. But I'll tell you what, I'm no match for you on a bronc." Might give him a run for his money on a bull though, although Jace wasn't going to bring that up yet.

Billy was appeased. He took his cell out of his pocket and called his mom. Willow tried her best to get the phone away from him.

"She wants to chew on it," he said while he waited for his mom to pick up.

"You get her over here as quick as you can, Billy, both her grandmas would love to spend the day with sweet Willow," they overheard Dottie's response.

"I'll run her over. Do you want to wait for me here, or should I meet you up at the mountain?" Billy asked Renie.

"I'll go with you," Jace offered.

A look passed between Blythe and Renie.

"Why?" Blythe asked.

"I'll let my mama and daddy know what I'm doing today. I'm feelin' kind of bad for leavin' without talking to them."

"Oh," Blythe frowned. "We don't have to go if you don't want to. I mean, we can go back to the house."

"What? I thought we were skiing today?" Renie pouted.

"We are," he answered. "Billy and I will be back as quick as we can. Blythe, can you call and reserve skis for us, since we won't be using theirs anymore?"

"Of course."

"Come, walk me out to the truck."

Blythe followed him, wondering what the hell was going on. This was turning into the most confusing morning.

"Listen, I want to give you some time alone with Irene. And I need to get to know Billy better. The thing between her and me is over. Now we need to learn how to be friends. Okay?"

"What about Tucker?"

"What's he got to do with this?"

"What if he wants to come back with you?"

Jace told her he'd already addressed the Tucker issue. He wasn't invited, and Jace had no intention of changing his mind about it.

"Public ski area," she murmured.

"He wants to show up on his own, that's his prerogative. But you and me...we're on a date."

The big smile he gave her went straight through her body, down to her toes. He was charm personified. His brother was, too. It dawned on her that those who played with fire often got burned. Was she getting too close to the flame with the Rice twins? As much as she wanted to have the upper hand, it was clear she didn't.

"Why did you wanna come with me?" Billy asked Jace once they were on the road.

"Those two have some stuff to work out. I figured they'd do it better without us around."

"Any other reason?"

"Yeah."

Billy waited for a few minutes, but Jace didn't continue. "You gonna tell me what it is?"

"Not sure how to say this without causing problems."

"Say it, for Christ's sake."

"Irene warned Blythe away from me."

Billy was quiet.

"Nothing to say?" Jace prodded.

"I'll handle it."

"I told her to back off, myself." Jace turned his head and looked out the window. "She's gotta get out of my business."

"I hear ya."

They spent the rest of the ride in silence.

"What about Tucker?" Renie asked Blythe once Billy and Jace were gone.

"I feel like it's a game."

"What do you mean?"

"It's a competition. It isn't about me; it's about which of them can win the girl."

"I don't know, Blythe. That doesn't sound like Jace."

"Maybe not Jace when he's alone. You haven't ever been around Tucker and him together, have you?"

Renie didn't answer, but it was a rhetorical question anyway. Blythe already knew the answer.

"I'm sure it's not as bad as you think."

She'd see, wouldn't she?

Tucker was sitting on the front porch, drinking coffee, when Jace and Billy drove up. He saw the question in Jace's eyes when he walked up.

"You kidnap her?"

"She's with Irene."

Billy got Willow out of her car seat and walked right past Tucker, without speaking.

"Mornin' to you, too," he said in the direction of the front door after it closed. "What's up his ass?"

"I told him somethin' that pissed him off on the way over here. Probably shouldn't have, but it's too late now."

"Jesus, Jace, we've been here less than twenty-four hours."

"It was about Irene. She told Blythe to stay away from me."

"Sound advice."

"I told her to back the hell off."

"And then you told the cowboy."

"Yep."

"Where are you taking her?"

"Blythe? We're goin' skiing."

Tucker looked away from him. "You have a good time, then."

"You okay?"

"Does it matter?"

"Come on, Tuck. I'm serious. Are you okay?"

Tucker didn't answer.

Billy came back out and walked toward the truck, and Jace followed. "Tell the parents we'll be back early this afternoon."

Tucker nodded and raised his coffee cup to his brother.

4

Jace was impressed. Blythe was a damn good skier. Irene was too, but she hung back with Billy, who appeared less angry once they got back to the house.

"Break?" he shouted to Blythe as they skied up to the lift line.

"Um, sure," she answered and skied toward the racks instead.

He picked up her skis after she released her boots from her bindings, and set them next to his. She handed him her poles, too.

"Having fun?" he asked.

"I am. You're good. Hard to keep up with."

"You shoulda said somethin', darlin'." Jace put his arm around her waist and pulled her closer to him. "I woulda slowed down for you."

She shifted away from him and walked toward the lodge.

"How about some hot chocolate?" he offered.

"Add some butterscotch schnapps to it and I'll be all in."

He smiled and went to the bar while she found them a table.

When he got back, she'd taken off her helmet and gloves, and was about to loosen her boots.

"Where'd you learn to ski, pretty girl?"

She grinned and rolled her eyes. "With my dad." She laughed. "You're *such* a cowboy."

"Now, why'd you say it that way, like it's a bad thing?"

"It's cute. That's what it is."

"Hey now, you don't call a cowboy cute, darlin'. Unless he's five years old."

He shifted his chair closer to her and put his arm around the back of hers. He turned so he was facing her.

"You know what they say about cowboys, don't ya?"

She laughed again. "No, I don't know what they say, and I'm not sure I want to."

"Better if I show you anyway." He leaned forward and brushed his lips over hers, just barely. He stopped, but didn't move away. Her eyes were closed and her cheeks were flushed.

"Jace—" she murmured.

"Shh now, I know what you're going to say."

"You do?"

"Yep. You're gonna say that we shouldn't do this, and then you're gonna say somethin' about Tuck. So before you do, let me remind you, I was the one who spoke first."

She nodded and smiled.

"Okay, then. Let's enjoy our date, darlin'. We'll see ol' Tuck at dinner. Until then, let's you and me put him out of our minds."

She nodded again, but her eyes were focused on his mouth. She gave him no choice, he had to kiss her. He put his hand around the back of her neck and held her still. He leaned forward and slowly brushed his lips over hers again. This time he didn't stop. When her lips opened to his, he seized the opportunity.

She was so soft and warm. He wanted her closer. He broke their kiss and pulled her toward him, off her chair and onto his lap. When her arms circled his shoulders, he kissed her again.

"I like kissin' you," he murmured against her lips.

She pulled back and took a deep breath, but stayed where she was, on his lap.

"There you are," said Renie. Billy was behind her and caught Jace's eye.

Blythe got up and sat back in her chair. "Hot chocolate break."

Billy pulled a chair out for Renie. "Looks like a little more than hot chocolate to me."

Blythe glared at him, and then looked at Renie, who was smiling. Thank God. She didn't want any crap from her today. She had her hands full between Jace and Tucker.

"Want some hot chocolate, darlin'?" Billy asked Renie, walking toward the bar before she had a chance to answer.

Blythe laughed.

"What's funny?" asked Jace.

"You two—with all your 'darlins' and 'pretty girls.' You're both such *cowboys*."

She looked over at Renie, who was still smiling.

"What's with you?" she asked.

"Nothing."

"Come on, Renie, speak. What's going on in that head of yours?"

"I'm happy."

"That's it? You're happy."

Blythe looked at Jace, who was looking at Renie, but turned to look at her. He smiled, too.

"I feel like there's something going on and no one is telling me what it is." It was beginning to irritate her.

Renie reached over and squeezed Blythe's shoulder. "Don't worry, nothing is going on. I mean it. I'm happy." Renie looked between Blythe and Jace, shook her head, and then looked toward the bar.

"I'm gonna go see if Billy needs any help."

"What was that about?" Blythe asked Jace once Renie was gone.

"I have *no* idea. But I get the impression she likes seein' the two of us together. Don't you?"

"I don't know what to think."

Jace didn't either. Irene's reaction was…unusual. Especially given it was such an abrupt departure from her attitude earlier. It didn't matter though. He liked Blythe. She was fun to be around, and he intended to be around her as much as possible.

"Where were we before they came in?" He pulled her back onto his lap. "I like you better closer." He reached up and pulled her hat off. She put her hand on his, trying to stop him.

"I wanna run my fingers through your hair, darlin'. Let go now." He eased her hat away from her hand and put it on the table.

"Hat hair," she said and blushed, like she was embarrassed.

It was such a simple thing, but that vulnerability did something to him. He shifted her so she couldn't feel his reaction to it. What was it about her that made him want to keep her feeling that way? Vulnerable. Shy. A little off kilter.

"So sweet," he whispered and kissed her again. "You wanna keep skiing, sweetheart, or should we find somethin' else to keep us busy?"

Renie and Billy came back to the table before Blythe had a chance to respond.

"I got a text from my mom," Renie said. "She wants to know when we're coming back to the house."

"Everythin' okay?" asked Billy.

Renie texted something back to her mom and waited for a response.

"Yeah, everything is fine, but they're wondering."

Jace looked at Blythe again, who still hadn't spoken. "I think we're ready to call it a day," he answered for both of them. "I'll go turn our skis in. You wanna get out of those boots, darlin'?"

Jace was asking her a question—something about her boots. She was in a daze, brought on by getting lost in kissing him, just like she had with Tucker. In fact, she wasn't sure which one she was kissing for a minute. They were so much alike, yet so different. *God,* what was she doing?

She nodded her head and stood. "Yeah, sure." She sat back on the chair and took off her boots.

Billy stood. "I'll help," he said and picked up her boots. "Jace, you go get the skis, and I'll meet you at the rental place."

"Are you okay?" Renie asked.

"What? Yeah, I'm fine. I got a little light-headed for a minute. Alcohol, altitude, and an overly affectionate cowboy will do it every time," she grinned.

"You two are cute together."

"Cute? What? Who are you?" Blythe looked at her. "Aren't you the person who told me to stay away from him yesterday?"

"I don't know. It's different now. He seems different."

"Who does? Jace?"

"Yes, of course, Jace. I don't know what it is, but I like it."

Blythe raised her eyebrows.

"No, not like that. I mean, I like him with you."

Blythe had a hard time believing it, but didn't say so. A minute later Jace walked back in, carrying her snow boots. When he handed them to her and she slipped her feet in them, they were warm. She looked at him questioningly.

"Boot warmers. I put them in while we were skiing, so they'd be warm when we got back."

Blythe looked at Renie and they both giggled.

"Oh, God," Jace groaned. "What now?"

"Cowboys," they answered in unison before they started giggling again.

"Call your brother," Jace's mom said a few minutes after they walked in the front door. "It's time he came back."

"Where is he?" Blythe asked.

"Out wandering," Jace answered. "He's not big on holidays. He usually disappears for most of the day."

"Why?"

It wasn't something Jace wanted to talk about, especially to Blythe. "I'll tell you later," he answered. Even though he had no intention of doing so.

Tucker saw the text from Jace, but wasn't ready to be around people yet. He supposed he should go back anyway. If he stayed out here any longer, he might not ever go back, and then instead of escaping everyone's attention, it would be spotlighted on him.

He took one last look at his drawing before he closed his sketchbook. He almost didn't recognize the woman he'd spent the last half hour drawing. She didn't look like the woman he'd started to draw—she'd morphed into someone else. Someone who looked more like Blythe than *her*.

God, he hated holidays, but this one, more than most. When he woke this morning, it wasn't the first thing he thought of. He thought about Blythe instead, and how it'd felt to hold her the night before.

When he'd gone upstairs to find she wasn't there, that she and Jace had left and no one knew where they were, his thoughts had turned inward. Back to *her*. Back to that night. He'd gone out on the porch to be alone, and then Jace came back, and told him they were going skiing.

Jace had asked if he was okay. Did he really need to ask? Of course he wasn't okay. Jace felt it. This wasn't something Tucker could bury deep enough for Jace not to feel it. There wasn't a deep, deep enough for this.

Mama's gonna send me lookin for you, Jace texted. *Heading back.*

Blythe didn't need to turn and look when Tucker walked in. She knew he had. She could feel him. Jace reached over and covered her hand with his, as though he felt her reaction. Her cheeks burned when she looked up at him. What was it about these two men? It was as though there was a current connecting the three of them.

She'd felt it with Tucker last night. It wasn't that they didn't need to speak, it was more that they shouldn't. What passed between them was more than words could communicate.

She felt the same way with Jace today. And now that Tucker was back, she felt it with both of them and wasn't sure she liked it.

When he walked past and brushed against her, his heat instantaneously spread throughout her body. She looked up, but he didn't look back, and Jace saw the whole thing—Blythe didn't need to look at him to know it.

"Dinner," Liv announced, and everyone made their way to the table. Blythe felt more as though she was floating than walking; she wasn't sure her feet even touched the ground. Jace pulled a chair out for her and sat to her right. Tucker sat in the chair on her left, and when he did, the feeling that spread over her made her lose her breath.

Jace covered her hand with his, but she didn't look at him. She looked at Tucker instead. He looked different today. His eyes were dark. Instead of green, they looked brown. His face was tight, like it had been the day before, when they first met. She'd seen his darkness then, and now it was back.

"Hi," she said softly, moving her hand away from Jace.

He turned to look at her, but didn't answer. Instead, he brushed her cheek with the back of his hand.

Blythe pushed the food around on her plate. She wasn't hungry. She looked across the table at her dad, who was questioning her with his eyes.

With so many people and conversations flying around the long table, she didn't feel the need to talk. Even if she had, she wouldn't have known what to say. Jace and Tucker were quiet too, but she could feel them on either side of her.

She was so uncomfortable, she wanted to leave the table. Worse, she wanted to leave Crested Butte, go home, and escape the heat emanating from these two men.

Jace put his arm across the back of her chair, and when he did, Tucker glared at him. It didn't deter him. Instead of moving his arm away, he reached farther and laid his hand possessively on her shoulder.

She wanted to shrug it away. She didn't want him touching her. She didn't want Tucker to touch her either.

Tucker looked at her plate. "Not hungry?" Those were the first words he'd spoken since he sat down at the table.

"I'm not," she murmured.

"Me either," she thought she heard him say, but he had cleaned his plate.

It was as though the three of them were frozen in silence—trapped in an air pocket of stifling tension.

"Jeez, look at the three of you. What happened, did somebody die?" her father asked. Blythe felt the already overpowering tension spread around the table. Her dad laughed, but it was too late; the words were already out there.

Tucker mumbled, "excuse me," and left the table.

"What?" asked Mark. "I was joking."

"It's okay," said Carol, Jace and Tucker's mom, who was sitting next to Mark. She patted his hand as she said it.

"So, somebody did die?"

"Mark, drop it," said Paige, giving her husband a stern look.

"I'm sorry. I didn't know."

"Stop," Paige said again.

"Who's ready for pie?" asked Liv. "Anybody?" She looked around the table, trying to draw attention away from Mark, who wasn't doing a very good job recovering his gaff.

Blythe got up in search of Tucker. She hadn't seen where he'd gone, so she went downstairs first, but didn't see him. When she turned to go back upstairs, Jace stopped her.

"He's gone."

"What do you mean, he's gone? Where did he go?"

"I'm not sure. He took the truck."

"What happened, Jace?"

Jace rubbed his hands over his face. "Blythe, I...it's a long story. One I'd rather not get into right now."

There was an ache in Blythe's chest she couldn't put a name to. Dread mixed with sorrow was as close as she could get.

Before Thanksgiving, Renie had talked Ben and the rest of the guys in CB Rice into playing at the Goat that night. The bar, owned by the Rice family, was an institution on Elk Avenue, the main drag in Crested Butte.

With Tucker gone, the mood was subdued.

Her dad sat in on a couple of songs, and when he wasn't, he danced with Blythe.

"My turn." Jace tapped her father on the shoulder. Mark stepped aside, and Jace wrapped his arm around her waist, pulling her in, close to him. He rested his cheek against her hair and breathed in the scent of her.

"I'm sorry about today."

"Why are you sorry?"

"Tucker..."

"Again, why are you sorry? Tucker was the one who disappeared without saying goodbye."

He didn't know what to say. He understood how Tucker was feeling, more than he wanted to. The guilt began to creep in again.

"Jace, are you okay?"

He knew she could feel the tension that was slowly spreading throughout his body. He'd hoped holding her would stop it from happening this time.

"Yeah, I'm okay."

She pulled back so she could look in his eyes, but he didn't want her to. Not tonight.

"Let me hold you, Blythe." He wrapped his arm around her waist a little tighter. He felt her breath catch as much as he heard it.

"It must be bad, whatever it is."

He couldn't answer her, but yes, it was bad.

The rest of the band took a break, but Ben stayed where he was, just him and his guitar. Every word he sang cut into Jace's heart. It was as if Ben knew what had happened, but Jace knew that wasn't possible. Nobody knew but him. Not even Tucker.

So don't fall in love, there's just too much to lose
If you're given the choice, then I beg you to choose
To walk away, walk away, don't let her get you.
I can't bear to see the same happen to you.
Please, don't be sad now, I really believe,
She was the greatest thing that happened to me.

5

It was January before Blythe heard from Jace again. She still hadn't heard from Tucker.

Jace rode back to Aspen with his parents the day after Thanksgiving. When they said goodbye, it was friendly, almost cordial, but lacking the enthusiasm he'd had for her before Tucker disappeared.

Renie asked her if Jace had commented on Tucker's strange behavior, but Blythe told her he hadn't wanted to talk about it.

The Cochrans spent Christmas in Monument. Liv and Ben brought Ben's sons over with them Christmas night, so they could spend the morning with their mother and her husband.

Blythe and her parents spent the day quietly. Her older sisters were both married to Air Force officers who were stationed outside of Colorado. Brooke, the oldest, was in Germany with her husband, Tom. Blythe's other sister, Bree, was the one she was closest to. She was in Northern California. Her husband, Zack, had been deployed and was in Afghanistan. Paige and Mark wanted her to come and spend the holidays with them, but Bree told them there was a chance Zack would make it home for Christmas, and if he did, she wanted to be there.

Billy and Renie were at the ranch in Black Forest, but Blythe didn't want to intrude on their time together. They saw each other between Christmas and New Year's Eve. Then Billy took Renie and Willow back to Crested Butte.

Blythe didn't recognize the phone number when the call came in. She considered letting it go to voicemail, but changed her mind. There was a chance, however remote, that it was Tucker, and if it was, she doubted he'd leave a message.

"Hey, it's Jace," he said when she answered.

"Oh. Hi. How are you?" She tried not to sound disappointed, but she was.

"I'm good. How 'bout you?"

"I'm good. Um...how's Tucker?"

Jace hesitated long enough that Blythe thought she'd made a mistake by asking. "He's back in Europe. I think he might be somewhere in France at this point, or back in Spain."

"Oh."

More silence.

"I'm calling because I'm going to the stock show, with Billy of all people," he laughed. "I wanted to see if we could get together while I'm in town."

"Sure. I'd like that."

Jace told her they'd be in Denver for six days. Maybe longer, depending on what happened at the show.

"What do you mean?"

"Well…you're not going to believe this, but Billy is my trainer."

"For what?"

"Saddle bronc riding."

"Huh?"

"I'm riding saddle broncs."

"I heard you the first time. Why?"

"Kind of a long story."

"Have you always done this?"

"No, I used to ride bulls," he answered. "Listen, I'll explain later. I've got to run now, but I want to see you, Blythe. Can I call you in a couple days?"

"Uh, sure. Of course. Bye, Jace."

Jace hadn't told anybody of his plans to get back into bull riding. He'd intended to tell Tucker, but his brother was gone when they got back from Crested Butte.

"Be in touch," was basically all Tuck had said. Jace knew better than to ask more than that.

Instead, he called Billy Patterson.

"You goin' back on the circuit?" Jace asked.

"Thinkin' about it, even if only to officially announce my retirement. Why do you ask? You hopin' I'll leave Renie here alone or somethin'?"

Jace laughed. "No, nothing like that. It's more that I'm thinkin' of goin' out myself."

"For what?"

"Bulls."

"Huh? Since when are you a bull rider?"

"You don't know much about me, do ya?"

"Can't say I ever wanted to. Still don't."

Jace told Billy that his dad had been a bull rider and his grandfather had been one, too. Jace had toured on the circuit at the same time Billy had. He wasn't as competitive on bulls as Billy was on broncs, so their paths had never crossed.

When Jace tore his ACL skiing, he figured his bull-riding career was over. He'd kept it quiet, but he'd been riding practice bulls for about a year. He also rode bareback as often as he could, getting his muscles to grip and release without relying on a rope or spurs.

"You know what I don't get," Billy said after listening to him talk for a while.

"What's that?"

"Why bulls? Why not broncs?"

"I don't know. I never thought about broncs."

"My dad was a bull rider, too. He retired before I came along. Riding broncs wasn't intentional, at least not with competin' in mind. Had a couple rough ones to break, and my dad saw somethin' in the way I road 'em. He said I was a natural. You've ridden all your life, haven't ya?" He didn't wait for Jace to answer. "You're ridin' now, a flat-back horse, I'd guess, if you're workin' your muscles for bulls. But what do I know?"

"What are you sayin', Billy." Trying to follow Billy's train of thought was like trying to follow a jackrabbit through a thicket.

"Get on some broncs for Christ's sake. What do ya think I'm sayin'? Jesus. How many bulls bucked ya off? You got noodles for brains?"

"I guess it's worth a try."

Jace spent most of December in Crested Butte. Ben Rice and his brothers were talking about getting into stock contracting, so they set up a practice area on the ranch, where he and Billy trained most every day.

He'd rented a studio apartment near the ski area in town, and no one, other than Billy and Irene, knew he was there.

Once he got in the saddle, getting back on bulls never entered his mind again.

Jace wasn't sure he'd be ready to compete in Denver, but he'd be Billy's travel partner, and part of his crew anyway. Billy was serious about his retirement, and this would be the beginning of his last season. Going to the National Western would give the two some time out on the road together, working and practicing.

When Jace told Irene he and Billy would be traveling together, she didn't believe him.

"But, he never travels with anybody."

"I don't know what to tell you darlin'. It was his idea, not mine."

"Huh," she answered, still looking perplexed.

"Isn't it weird?" Blythe asked Renie when she told her what had been going on for the past few weeks with Jace and Billy.

"It was at first, but now it isn't. They're a lot alike. They still bicker all the time, if I didn't know better, I'd think they hated each other. But whatever. It works for them."

"Is Jace any good?"

"Better than he thinks. That's why Billy wants him to go to the stock show. Jace may be a full-time bronc rider a lot sooner than he thinks."

"I can't wait to see you," Blythe said, and meant it. The whole thing with Tucker had thrown her. She wished there was someone willing to tell her what his story was, but other than Jace, she didn't know anyone who knew any more than she did. She'd asked Renie to ask Ben, but he had no idea, and didn't offer to ask his aunt and uncle about it.

"Is Jace staying with you and Billy at the ranch in Black Forest during the stock show?"

"Yeah, there's plenty of room, so it would be silly for him to stay anywhere else. I still don't understand why he got his own place in Crested Butte when he could've stayed with my mom and Ben."

"You have no idea why he got a place of his own?" Blythe laughed.

"No. Why do you think he did?"

"Come on, Renie. You don't think Jace spends very many nights alone, do you?"

"Oh. I hadn't thought of that."

Blythe laughed again. Jace probably had a revolving door of cowgirls keeping him company in Crested Butte.

"What's going on with you and school, Renie? Are you goin' back?" she asked, wanting to change the subject.

"Yep, so I'll be home more often than I am now. It's going to be so hard to be away from Willow, but I only have one more year of school left, so Billy thinks I should just get it done and over with now. Plus Billy said that he and Willow would stay with me in Fort Collins as much as they could during the week."

"So, you'll be here on the weekends?"

"I sure will. It'll be just like old times."

Blythe didn't say it, but it wouldn't be like old times at all, not now that Renie was not only a mom, but practically a married woman too."

"Will Billy have to work after he retires?" Blythe asked.

"Sort of. I think he's been talking to Ben about partnering in a rough stock contracting business."

"What's that?"

"You know how every rodeo has bulls and broncs for the cowboys to compete on?"

"Yeah."

"Well, stock contractors are the ones who supply them."

"Do they get paid?"

"Oh, yeah." Renie laughed. "They get paid a lot."

Blythe had never known much about Billy's financial situation, but it had always been obvious his family didn't hurt for money. Other than working on the ranch and traveling to rodeos, she'd never known Billy to do anything else. Renie had said something about investments the family had in oil, somewhere up north, but Blythe hadn't paid much attention when Renie told her. Obviously he had enough money to buy Liv's ranch, along with a very nice house in Crested Butte, and rent a place in Fort Collins.

Blythe didn't have the luxury of a flush bank account. Her parents had been patient with her, but she could tell it was wearing thin. Her mother started suggesting different career fields she might be interested in. So far, she'd given her brochures on becoming a home health-care aide, a dental technician, and a computer programmer. None appealed to her. She'd hated the nursing program she'd been in so much, she quit. Any job in a medically-related field was out as far as she was concerned and sitting in front of a computer, writing code, sounded like the most boring thing she could imagine.

She'd been working at the tea house in downtown Monument since right before Christmas. The people who owned it were very nice, as was everyone else who worked there. She enjoyed it, despite her mother's nagging that she wasn't being sufficiently challenged.

Now that Renie was going to finish her degree, Blythe knew her mother's pressure would intensify.

"My mom and Ben are coming to town for the stock show, too," Renie told her. "I think they'll be staying with you and your parents."

"How's your mom feeling?"

"She feels great, and she looks even better. She says it's a girl glow."

"She's having a girl?"

"She thinks so, but they haven't found out for sure. Ben isn't too excited about it."

"Why not?"

"He says he doesn't know how to raise girls."

"Have him talk to my dad."

"I think he did, and your dad said that at least Ben has two sons and some other testosterone around, unlike him who's still the only guy in your house."

"That's right. Even our dog is a girl."

Blythe hadn't wanted to say goodbye, but Renie told her Willow had just woken up from her nap, so she had to go.

She couldn't imagine not being able to finish a telephone conversation because of a baby. It would be a long, long time before she'd be ready to let go of her freedom the way Renie had.

Jace called the day before the stock show opened, and asked if he could see her that night. He'd said he still wanted to see her once the show opened, but he wouldn't have as much free time.

Blythe was a nervous wreck, waiting for him to get to the house. A couple of times she thought about texting him and canceling, but she and Renie had plans to be at the show every day Billy and Jace were in town, so it would've been awkward to see him after begging off their date.

When he got there, she invited him in, but an hour later, she wished she hadn't. Jace fit in so well with her parents and Ben and Liv, she wondered if he remembered she was there.

Lost in thought, feeling ignored, she checked Facebook on her phone. When she looked up, Jace was watching her. He smiled.

"You ready to go, darlin'?"

"Sure. I mean, if you still want to. We could hang out here if you'd rather."

Jace stood in front of her. "Of course I still want to spend the evening with you, sweet girl. I was trying to make a good impression on your parents, but I neglected you in the meantime, didn't I?"

She shrugged, not wanting to admit she'd been feeling sorry for herself.

"C'mon, let's get outta here."

"Where are we going?" she asked once they were in his truck.

"I have options for you. Either St. Augustine Grille or the Castle Café. What's your pleasure, darlin'?"

That was a tough decision. Both were in Castle Rock, about twenty minutes north of Monument. The Castle Café was more casual and St. Augustine Grille was definitely more romantic. She hated being the one to decide where to eat. Renie knew that about her and never made her pick. When she went out with Tucker, he hadn't even asked.

"Oh my," Jace said, touching her chin. "You're workin' quite a pout over there. You want me to choose, Blythe?"

"Yes. You pick. Either one is okay with me."

He didn't say anything else during the drive. When he pulled up across the street from the grille, she grinned, happy he chose romance.

"Figured I dropped the ball, wooin' you at Thanksgiving. Maybe you'll let me give it another try. Whaddaya say?"

She smiled, but didn't answer, which seemed to make him happy.

Over dinner he told her about training with Billy, and she asked him if it was weird, like she'd asked Renie.

"Nah. I was over Renie by the time I met you, Blythe."

She raised her eyebrows.

"Okay, maybe not over her, but resigned to her bein' with Billy. No point beating a dead horse, if ya know what I mean."

Jace leaned closer and covered her hand that was resting on the table with his. "I don't want to talk about Renie, darlin'. I want to talk about you."

"I'm not as interesting as Renie is." She tried not to sound as though she was feeling sorry for herself again, because it was true. Compared to the rest of the people she hung around with, she didn't have much going on in her life.

"You sell yourself short, Blythe."

"Oh, yeah? Tell me, then, what do you find interesting about me?"

He said she was beautiful and nice to talk to, and then she stopped listening, and started thinking about Tucker.

There hadn't been a minute in the time she spent with him when she hadn't believed he found her fascinating, or that she hadn't felt like the center of his attention. Jace reminded her of boys she'd dated in high school. He was hot as all get out, funny, charming, and flirtatious, but there was something missing. She wouldn't have known to even look for it if she hadn't felt it with Tucker.

"Have you been to the Next Door Bar?" she asked as they were leaving the restaurant.

"No, where is it? Next door?"

She laughed. "Not next door to here. It's actually next door to Castle Café."

"Let's do it. Can we walk from here?"

"Definitely," she answered. "What happened, Jace?"

"With Tuck?"

"Yeah." She couldn't stop herself from asking. He'd been on her mind all night. Jace had to have sensed it.

"I figured you'd ask at some point." He rubbed his face with his hands again, as he'd done the last time she asked him about him.

"It isn't my story to tell, Blythe. Tuck…God, I'm so uncomfortable. He should tell you. Not me."

Blythe put her hand on his arm and stopped him. "It's okay," she said. "You don't have to tell me."

"I'm sorry, Blythe. I can't talk about it."

"Like I said, it's okay. Let's change the subject."

They walked to the bar in silence, but once they were inside, the music and crowd distracted them. They danced and talked more about rodeo. There were a lot of cowboys in the bar, and soon Jace got involved in a conversation about the stock show. When he mentioned he was traveling with Billy Patterson, people started asking about him.

"Billy's a rock star," said the girl sitting next to Blythe at the bar.

"Yeah, even outside the rodeo he is," answered Blythe, laughing.

"I'm Lyric," she introduced herself. "I'm the host of RodeoChat."

"Blythe, I...uh...don't know that much about rodeo. I mean, I've been a few times, but that's it."

"No matter. It's nice to meet you, Blythe. Pretty good lookin' cowboy you're out with tonight."

Blythe looked over at Jace. Good looking didn't begin to describe him. He was beautiful. He'd let his blond hair grow out since the last time she saw him, although she heard him ask her dad if there was a place where he could get a haircut tomorrow. If she remembered later, she'd try to talk him out of it. She liked the way it curled against the collar of his shirt.

He looked over at her and smiled. When he saw she was talking to Lyric, he winked, and then went back to his conversation with the guys.

Lyric fanned herself when he did. "God, he's hot. What color are his eyes? Green? He doesn't have a brother does he?"

Blythe laughed again. "He does. A twin, in fact."

"Oh my 'lanta," said Lyric. "Is he here, too?"

No, he was in Europe—that's what Jace had said. She wished she could see him, talk to him, get him to tell her what the big secret was. Obviously it was something important, life-changing and traumatic, given his reaction on Thanksgiving.

"I'm a twin, too. How 'bout that? I have a twin brother." When Blythe didn't answer, Lyric asked if she was okay.

"Yeah. Sorry. No, his brother isn't here. He's in Europe."

Lyric tilted her head and looked at her as though she expected Blythe to keep talking.

"He's a nice guy, too," was all she said.

"Hmm, sounds like there's a story there."

"There is," Blythe answered. "But I don't know it."

"Speaking of stories, I'd love to interview Billy Patterson on RodeoChat. Think you can hook me up?"

"What's RodeoChat?"

Lyric explained that she hosted social media interviews with people in the rodeo industry. Blythe wasn't sure, but she thought she might be able to get Billy to do an interview. Lyric asked more questions, and before she knew it, Blythe had told her the whole story of Billy, Renie, and Willow. It dawned on her suddenly that she shouldn't have.

"Don't worry," said Lyric, sensing her discomfort. "If I get the chance, I'll keep my questions focused on his career as a saddle bronc champion. I'll keep his personal life out of it, unless he brings it up himself."

"Thanks," said Blythe. "Either you're way too easy to talk to or these Jack and cokes are going down a little too fast. I ran off at the mouth more than I should have."

"It's okay," said Lyric. "I won't tell anyone else, I promise."

Blythe hoped so. Lyric seemed trustworthy. Although, her dad told stories of how he'd gotten in trouble with the media back when he was on tour with his band.

"My dad used to get in a lot of trouble *over-talking*." Blythe laughed. "He was in a band."

"What band?

"Ever heard of Cochran?"

"Of course, I have."

"Cochran's our last name, and the name of his band."

"You're not going to believe this," said Lyric. "My dad was in Satin. He still is, but they don't tour as much as they used to."

"This is wild. I know Satin. My dad would freak out right now. I have to text him. What's your dad's name?"

Blythe texted her dad, and as she predicted, he was ready to jump in the car and drive up to meet Lyric. Blythe told him not to, but it would be just like him to do it anyway.

"It just dawned on me, your name, Lyric…it's very symbolic, isn't it?"

She laughed. "Yeah, my parents were…like that. My brother's name is Bullet."

"Seriously? Sounds like there's a story there," she laughed, repeating what Lyric had said earlier. "No story here. I'm named after Blythe Danner, not symbolic at all."

"That's cool."

"How did you get into rodeo if you were raised by a rocker?"

"My grandma was a barrel racer back in the day. I spent a lot of time with her when I was growin' up—with my dad on tour and all. Once I got a little older, my mama went with him. Anyway, my grandma took me to rodeos all the time."

"And you turned it into a career."

"As I got older, I started payin' more attention and realized there wasn't a place where you could real-time results for anything other than the big rodeos. You can't even get those all the time. So, I started RodeoChat on social media, to have a place for folks to find out results, chat about rodeo, that kind of stuff."

"Smart."

"Smart or crazy, not sure which," Lyric laughed. "It isn't the only thing I do."

"What else do you do?"

"I still work in the music biz."

"Still?"

"Yeah, I've been workin' with my grandma as long as I can remember. She owns a talent agency."

"Wow, that's big."

Lyric laughed again. "Yeah, it's big, but that isn't all I do."

"It isn't?"

"Nah. I'm also a vet tech, although I don't have as much time to do that as I'd like."

"You're kidding. How old are you?"

When Lyric told her she was her age, Blythe wanted to crawl into a hole.

"You've done so much with your life, and me? I haven't done jack shit with mine."

"Well, maybe you oughta find somethin' that interests you."

"Easier said than done. Anyway, let's change the subject back to the vet business. Renie, the one I was telling you about, who's engaged to Billy, she's going to CSU to get a degree as a large animal vet."

"Cool! That'll give me more to talk to her and Billy about. You're awesome, Blythe."

"I don't know about that. I have awesome friends, that's the extent of my awesomeness."

"I don't believe that for a minute. You'll figure it out. I got a feelin' about you."

Jace watched Blythe talk to the girl at the bar. It looked like they were having a good time. He'd started to feel guilty about talking with the guys, but every time he looked over she was talking and smiling.

He walked over to where she sat, stood behind her, and put his arm around her waist.

"Havin' a good time, darlin'?"

"I am. This is Lyric. Lyric this is Jace Rice."

"Nice to meet you, Jace. I was trying to talk Blythe into getting me an interview with Billy Patterson. Maybe you can help me with that."

"Lyric, such a unique name. It sounds familiar—"

"RodeoChat," she answered before he could ask.

"That's right. Lyric. Wow! It's nice to meet you. I've seen some of your interviews. Good stuff. And yeah, I'm sure Billy would be willing."

"Cool! I'm gonna get goin'. Big week ahead of me an' all. It was great talkin' to you, Blythe. Will you be up at the National Western?"

"All week," Jace answered for her.

Lyric handed her a card. "This has my cell number on it. Call me tomorrow, okay? I wanna talk to you more, Blythe. I've got some ideas I wanna run by you."

"Me? Uh, okay. I'm not sure why you'd want to talk to me, but yeah, I'll call you."

"You made a friend," Jace said, whisking her out on the dance floor just in time for a slow song.

"She was fun to talk to. I hope Billy isn't mad at us for practically committing him to an interview."

"Nah, he won't be. Don't you worry." Jace pulled her closer and breathed in her scent. She smelled like vanilla and fresh air. He nuzzled closer. "I missed you, Blythe."

He felt her shoulders tense. "You don't believe me?"

"I must've missed all those messages you left me," she mumbled.

"I haven't talked to anybody since Thanksgiving."

"Nobody? What about Billy? And *Renie?*"

"Ah, there we go. Now we get to what's really bothering you. You have no reason to be jealous of Irene."

"Who says something is bothering me? And who says I'm jealous?"

"You do. Come on now, let me make it up to you."

The longer they danced, the more Jace wanted to kiss her. He waited, though. He wanted to be alone with her when he did. Not on a crowded, noisy dance floor. Maybe instead of staying with Billy and Renie, he should reserve a hotel room in Denver.

"Jace, I'm not sure—"

"Shh, don't say it."

"You don't even know what I'm going to say."

"I think I do."

"He's here with us whether you want him to be or not."

It didn't matter whether Blythe was with Tucker or Jace, the other was always there, too. She wondered if it would always be that way. Eventually, maybe she'd see them as individuals, separate from one another.

She shouldn't have brought Tucker up, since Jace was being so nice, but she couldn't help it. There was something about him that stuck with her. If she'd predicted which of the Rice brothers she'd hear from again, she would've said Tucker, not Jace.

"You can't stop thinkin' about him."

"No. I can't. I'm sorry. I'm worried about him."

"He's okay, Blythe. It's somethin' he has to work through, and he's gotta do it on his own."

"But—"

"It happened a few years ago. It's his damage, darlin'. There isn't anything you or I can do for him. Not until he decides he's ready."

"You're still not going to tell me what happened?"

"No, I'm not. It's up to him to tell you, Blythe. I'm sorry."

They danced through the end of the song, and before Blythe could ask, he motioned toward the door.

"Why don't you wait here? I'll go get the truck."

"No, it's okay. I'd like to walk."

"Okay, if that's what you want to do."

He held her hand once they got outside, and then pulled her closer and put his arm around her.

"Give me a chance, Blythe, please," he whispered. When she turned to answer, he gripped her face and covered her mouth with his.

Just like when he'd kissed her at the ski area, she felt funny after talking about Tucker, but the longer his tongue did battle with hers, the less she wanted him to stop, and the more his brother faded to the back of her mind.

He pushed her against the brick side of the building, put his hands inside her jacket, and eased them under her sweater. He cupped each side of her waist and moved higher, until his hands rested under the curve of her breasts. When his thumbs brushed her nipples, she felt heat spread through the rest of her body. She pushed into him, kissing him harder.

Jace rested his forehead against hers but left his hands where they were. "I wanna be alone with you, Blythe, so bad. But…"

The sound of his voice broke through the haze of his kiss, and she pushed away from him. "I can't do this, Jace. I'm sorry."

"Who are you thinking about instead of me, Blythe? Is it Tucker, or are you still worried about—"

She put her fingers over his lips. She didn't want to hear him say Renie's name. "Take me home, Jace."

Jace held her hand in his and ran his thumb back and forth over her knuckles, but Blythe was lost in thought on the drive home. She hummed along with the music on the radio, but he doubted she knew she was doing it.

She took a deep breath and rested her head against the window. He'd give anything to know what she was thinking about. Although he had a pretty good guess.

6

Dottie and Bill, Billy's parents, were keeping Willow with them so Renie could go to the stock show with Blythe. Ben and Liv were going too, but driving separately.

"It's been a long time since we went to the rodeo," Renie said on the way there.

"A very long time. Guess we won't be checkin' out the cowboys, the way we used to."

Blythe wondered if Renie had ever checked out other cowboys. From what she'd said in the last couple of months, she'd been in love with Billy Patterson long before she and Blythe went to their first rodeo.

"What about you? Are you and Jace...you know?"

"Are we what?"

"Seeing each other?"

"I'm not sure, to tell you the truth." She still couldn't stop thinking about Tucker, but she'd given the situation a lot of thought last night. Tucker was gone, and Blythe didn't know if she'd ever see him again. Jace was here, and interested. Maybe she should give him the chance he was asking for.

"Billy wondered. He asked me this morning when Jace told him he'd decided to stay in Denver the rest of the week."

"Interesting," she grinned. "Well, it *is* a long ride home every night."

Blythe started to giggle and Renie joined her.

* * *

Tucker knew he was being an asshole when he up and left the dinner table on Thanksgiving. He hadn't intended to leave, necessarily. He went outside, hoping to shake off the ghosts, but they wouldn't let loose. What started out as a drive to clear his head, ended up taking him back over the pass and home. He hadn't even taken the time to thank Ben and Liv for inviting him to dinner.

More importantly, he hadn't said goodbye to Blythe. Sitting on the beach in San Sebastian, he had little recollection of how he got back to Spain, but the memory of Blythe Cochran remained crystal clear.

He'd been in the seaside community for over a month, painting. He had few pieces to show for it in terms of the Basque landscape. Blythe, on the other hand, he could paint all day.

When he got the email from Jace, saying he was competing in the National Western, riding saddle broncs of all things, he figured the next thing he'd read would be that he was seeing Blythe. Sure enough, the next paragraph said he hadn't seen or talked to her since the day after Thanksgiving, but he planned to while he was in Denver.

His gut twisted when he read it. Here he was, five thousand miles away, and he'd been the one who put himself here. Every night, he dreamed about her. When he was awake, all he had to do was close his eyes, and there she was. One ghost had been replaced by another, but this ghost he could talk to, wrap his arms around, and sink his body into. And yet, he wasn't doing any of those things.

***

Blythe sent a text to Lyric when she and Renie got to the show complex.

"I can't wait for you to meet her," she told Renie. "She's super fun to talk to. She and I hit it off right away."

Renie was sullen, and then suddenly, she wasn't anymore.

"What just happened?"

"I have to get used to sharing," she answered. "I'm not very good at it."

Blythe laughed. That was one of the most honest things she'd ever heard her friend say. "Good job," she finally was able to say between giggles. "You're workin' that say-what-you-think thing. I'm proud of you."

Lyric texted back, and they arranged a place and time to meet. "Oh, I forgot to mention, she wants to interview Billy for RodeoChat." Blythe hoped Jace had mentioned it to him. She'd forgotten all about it.

"Hey, Blythe," Lyric came bounding up to them and hugged her hello.

"Sorry," Lyric said when Blythe stiffened. "Sometimes I'm a little overenthusiastic. Plus, I don't know what it is, Blythe, but I feel like I've known you forever."

Renie was making that face again, the one where she looked like she'd taken a bite of lemon. Blythe elbowed her in the side.

"Lyric, this is my life-long best friend, Renie. Renie, this is my new best friend, Lyric."

The smile Renie had recovered with her introduction quickly faded.

"You're the one who's engaged to Billy Patterson, and a large animal vet."

Lyric linked arms with Renie, and from that moment on, the two had one another's undivided attention. Blythe wondered if there would be any questions left to ask Billy or if Renie had already answered them. The best part of it, though, was that Renie had warmed up to Lyric and she wasn't mad anymore.

"Where are ya'll sitting?" Lyric asked. When Renie told her, she invited them to join her instead. "Mine are a whole lot better than yours," Lyric held up her press pass. "I can go just about anywhere."

Blythe thought their seats were pretty good, considering they'd gotten them from Billy, who was a former NFR saddle bronc champion.

"Oh, I meant to tell you, when I was walkin' through the parking lot a few minutes ago, I think I saw your cowboy's twin. Looked just like him, but with longer hair."

Blythe grabbed Renie's arm and steadied herself.

"Are you okay?" Lyric asked.

"She's fine," Renie answered for her. "Um, she hasn't seen him in a while, and I think you surprised her."

"But wait, aren't you datin' the other one? The one I met you with."

Blythe didn't know where to begin, and even if she did, she wasn't sure she'd regained the ability to speak. Had Jace known Tucker was going to be here and didn't tell her? They'd talked about him last night. Why wouldn't Jace have said something then?

She looked around the arena, but instead of finding Tucker, she saw Jace. His brow furrowed and he squinted his eyes. "What's up?" he mouthed. He pulled out his cell phone and held it up.

Tucker, she texted.

What about him?

He's here.

Jace didn't need to answer her text for her to know that he was surprised.

Tucker was beginning to think he'd made a mistake by not getting in touch with Jace. He was able to get into the stock show, but the rodeo was sold out. He pulled out his phone to text him and saw he'd missed a call and a text from him.

Where are you?

Here. Rodeo sold out. Can't get in.

Meet me at back entrance near barns.

Tucker had an overpowering feeling Jace was not happy he was here. As he walked toward the barns and caught sight of his brother's face, his feeling was confirmed.

"What are you doing here?"

"That's a nice greeting."

"Answer me."

"What's your fuckin' problem, Jace? Jesus—I'm here to see you ride."

"Bullshit. Try again. What are you doin' here?"

There was no point in answering him. He was right. Maybe in part it was to see his brother, but it was a very small part. He was here to see Blythe, and Jace knew it.

"Where is she?"

Jace walked away without answering. When Tucker didn't follow, Jace turned around. "Did you wanna get into the rodeo or not?"

Jace flashed his credentials at the cowgirl sitting by the door. The look on her face let them know they could've gotten in without any problem, credentials or not.

"Where is she?" Tucker asked again.

"What makes you think she's here?"

"She's here."

There were so many things Jace wanted to say to Tucker, and all of them would be said in anger. He was as mad at himself as he was at his brother, though. He'd been the dumbass who'd told Tuck that he planned to see Blythe. He might as well have waved a red cape in front of one of the bulls. Of course, that got Tucker on the next plane. *Of course.* Why had he been so stupid?

Last night, he'd practically begged Blythe to give him a chance to make her forget about Tucker. Now, the only chance he had was a fat one.

Blythe's view was unobstructed when she saw Jace come through the door with Tucker, who followed his brother's gaze and looked straight at her. And damn him, he smiled. She couldn't help herself; she smiled back.

The roar of the crowd in the arena had quelled to background noise. Everything else but Tucker faded away.

"*Holy shit,*" she heard someone say. It might've been Lyric. "Damn, those two are hot."

"Mmm hmm," Blythe murmured. It was precisely what she thought when they'd climbed out of the truck, the first time she saw them.

They looked so much alike—yet so different. Jace was all cowboy tonight. Tucker, on the other hand, had on a dark turtleneck sweater, which, from a distance, looked rich and soft. He moved with perfect grace in his snug jeans, and while she couldn't tell from where she was, she guessed he had on the same black boots he was wearing when she met him.

He looked like an artist, or maybe a writer. At the same time, he fit in perfectly in the rodeo setting. He moved with the ease of a man accustomed to being around rough stock.

Her gaze shifted to Jace, who looked as though he'd been able to read her thoughts and knew they had nothing to do with him. Disappointment carved grooves in his brow; his eyes darkened and lost their fire.

Blythe wanted to comfort him, tell him it would be okay, but the man standing next to him made that impossible. Even from a hundred feet away, Blythe was willing to do whatever Tucker asked of her. No one had ever affected her this way. Not even Jace.

There she was. Not close enough to touch, but almost. Tucker wanted to jump the fence and walk straight through the arena to her, but he couldn't get his body to move. It was as though a part of him was acutely aware that, once he moved, once he walked to where she was, once he touched her, his life and hers would irrevocably change.

His face still held a smile. He couldn't help himself; seeing her made him happy. And she smiled back. How long had they been staring at each other from this distance? Not so long that her eyes showed doubt. They still held his, transfixed.

He kept his gaze on her while he weaved his way in and out of the crowd. She stood and walked in his direction. God, he liked that about her, that she wouldn't simply stand and wait. She'd come to him, too.

It was all she could do not to run. It was too crowded to, but that's what her body longed to do. The walk to him seemed impossibly long.

He was still a few feet away when she stopped. *What was she doing?* This was not a long lost lover or even a dear friend. This was not a long lost lover or even a dear friend. This was a man she'd had dinner with once, then he left and hadn't said goodbye. She hadn't heard a word from him since. What was she thinking? She shook her head and turned to go back to her seat.

She stopped. Why? And worse, instead of coming to him, she was walking away. Tucker worked his way through the last of the crowd that separated them and grabbed her arm, right above her elbow.

"Blythe?"

She jerked her arm away. "I can't do this."

A wall of people trying to move through the coliseum prevented her from getting any farther away from him. Tucker stood behind her and put his hand on her waist. "I'm sorry," he whispered.

He felt her body tense. Her breathing accelerated. "What for?" she asked.

"Everything," he answered.

"Let go of me, Tucker" she cried, but at the same time, leaned back into him.

When she did, he wrapped his arm further around her waist and held on tight. "Don't walk away from me," he murmured.

"You can't do this. Jace—"

"He knows why I'm here."

Tucker maneuvered her out of the crowd and off to the side, out of the way of the mass of people.

He spun her around against the tile wall, bringing his hand up to caress her face. He'd been dreaming about this too long. It was time to make his dreams a reality. He looked into her eyes, which were darting back and forth between his and his mouth.

"Blythe," he said again before he covered her lips with his. His other arm wrapped around her waist, and he held her as close to him as he could.

She wasn't fighting against him—she wasn't trying to stop their kiss. Slowly, the hands that had been stiff against him held on tight instead. She gripped the front of his shirt, digging her fingers into his chest.

"Come on," he said, pulling her toward the door leading outside the coliseum.

"No," she might not be able to resist him, but she was *not* leaving. "I'm here to watch Billy and Jace ride. I'm not going anywhere with you. If you want to see me, you'll have to stay here."

He grinned. "Oh yeah? You puttin' your foot down?"

She smiled. She didn't want to, but when Tucker did, she couldn't help herself. When he went from thundercloud broody to hot as the summer sun, there was nothing she could do but melt under the heat of him.

"Yeah," she answered. "I am." She shimmied away from him but took his hand as she did.

"Where you takin' me, girl?"

"We have an extra seat. It's your lucky night," she murmured.

He released her hand as they merged into the crowd and planted his hands on her hips. He held on tight, and when she turned, his hand cupped her bottom. When she swatted at him, he squeezed tighter.

"You want my hands all over you, don't you, Blythe?"

"I see you didn't leave your arrogance in Spain."

He laughed. Blythe pushed his buttons, every one of them, in all the right ways.

"You remember Renie," Blythe said when they got to the seats. "And this is Lyric Simmons."

Tucker was polite and said hello, but his gaze lingered on Blythe. Even when they sat, he couldn't look away. He'd pictured her in his mind; he'd painted her from his memory, but now she was next to him. He wanted to do nothing but soak in the sight of her.

"You're making me uncomfortable," she whispered.

"I don't care." His eyes trailed from hers, over her body. "You wouldn't leave with me, so you'll have to deal with the fact that I can't take my eyes off of you. I thought about you every minute, Blythe. Every minute."

Her eyes closed, longer than a blink. Her cheeks flushed. He leaned over and put his lips where he watched the pulse of her heart beating, stronger and stronger the more he said.

"Oh my God," she groaned. "You've made your point." She moved away from him. "I told you I'm not leaving until Billy and Jace have ridden. The minute they have, we can go. Good enough?"

He answered her with a kiss—deep and hot enough that he was sure he was making everyone around them as uncomfortable as he was making her. He didn't care.

7

Jace wanted to slam his hand into the nearest wall, but it was concrete, so he pulled his punch right before it made contact. *Goddamn Tucker.*

Part of him wanted to storm out, throw his hands in the air, and quit. But that wasn't who he was. He'd wanted to ride for Blythe tonight, show her how hard he'd been working at this. Make her proud. Now he doubted she'd be paying attention anyway.

What was wrong with him? Why had he told Tucker he planned to see her?

"How ya doin' there, *Romeo*?"

"Fuck off, Billy."

"Couple rabbits over there checkin' you out."

"I mean it, Patterson, leave me the hell alone."

Billy slugged him. "We gotta get you a woman, Rice. You've been strikin' out on yer own. I'll see if I can help ya out."

Tucker felt Jace's pain strongly enough that he eased away from their kiss. Worse, though, Blythe had seen the look on his brother's face, and it had devastated her.

He knew the minute, the very instant, she realized how much they'd hurt him.

She'd gotten up and hurried off before Tucker realized what was happening. By the time he got up to follow her, she was far enough ahead of him that he couldn't catch her before she slipped into the ladies' room.

He'd been standing near the door long enough to worry she'd stay in there the rest of the night. He thought about asking one of the women going in, to check on her, but what could he say? He was tempted to go in after her himself.

"Hey," she said, finally coming back out.

"Hey. You okay?"

"No. I'm not. What're you gonna do about it? Anything?"

He laughed. He couldn't help it.

"It isn't funny, Tucker. You know what else? You're a shitty brother."

He shrugged outwardly, but inside he knew she was right.

"This is Jace's night, not yours. Is this the way it's always been with you two?"

Tucker didn't know what to say. He didn't think so, but maybe it was.

"You know how I feel, don't you?" she asked.

"I think so," he said, but he wasn't sure exactly what she was referring to. Was she talking about how she felt about him or about the situation with Jace or something else?

"Why did you leave?"

He was afraid that was what she meant, as much as he hoped she wouldn't go there. "It's complicated."

"Why did you leave?"

"I already answered that question."

"No, you didn't. You have serious problems, Tucker. If you're unwilling to talk to me about them, then I can't get involved with you. I mean, you just got up and left in the middle of Thanksgiving dinner. What the hell?"

"It was what your dad said."

"Now this is my dad's fault." She turned to walk away.

"Wait," he grabbed her arm. "That isn't what I meant."

She pulled her arm away. "I'm getting tired of you grabbing me. Don't do that. If I walk away, you can either let me go, or you can follow me, but *quit* grabbing at me."

He held both hands in the air.

"I don't even know you," she stammered.

"Yes, you do. And what's more, you want to know me better."

"I don't think I do, and I'm not being a smart ass when I say that."

"You can't help yourself any more than I can."

"I don't know, Tucker. It would be so much easier to walk away, find another guy who doesn't have a twin brother, for one. Someone who doesn't have so many damn problems."

Tucker and Blythe's phones both pinged at the same time. If they hadn't, neither might have looked. But it was Jace and he was getting ready to ride. He wanted to know if either one of them were still there.

Blythe stormed off, leaving Tucker unsure of which way he should go. There was one thing she'd been right about, he was a shitty brother. Instead of following her, Tucker went in the direction of the chutes.

Blythe got back to her seat in time to see Jace lowering himself on the back of the bronc. She held her breath as she waited for him to signal that he was ready for his crew to pull the door of the chute open.

Lyric leaned over. "Marking out is the first step. Do you know what that is, Blythe?"

God, she could kiss Lyric. That would certainly solve some of her problems, but this was for a different reason. Blythe had no idea what to look for, and Lyric was going to explain it to her.

"He has to have both spurs touching the bronc above the point of the horse's shoulder on its first jump out of the bucking chutes. If he doesn't, he won't get a score."

"Then what?"

"Then he has to time his movements with the horse's jumps. He'll need to move his feet in an arc from the horse's shoulders back to the saddle skirt. The more even and accurate his movements, the more points he'll earn. Course, he's gotta stay on for eight seconds, if he gets bucked off, none of the rest matters."

"Thanks, Lyric."

When the chute opened, Jace looked like he was in the right position based on what Lyric told her. Blythe couldn't tell if he was doing the rest of what she'd said; she only watched the clock. Six, seven, eight seconds… the pickup men scooped him off and he was on the ground, celebrating.

Blythe jumped up and down, clapping her hands. Renie let out a loud whistle, and Lyric was hooting and hollering. He saw her, she was sure of it. He knew she'd watched him ride.

Tucker made her blood boil, but Jace—he melted her heart. She'd never feel about him the way that she did about Tucker, but it didn't matter. In that moment, she knew exactly what she had to do.

By the time the excitement died down and anyone was paying attention, Blythe was gone. They'd assume she went to see Jace, or to find Tucker, but she wasn't doing either.

"What do you mean she's not with you, Renie?"

"I thought she was coming down here."

Jace ran his hand through his hair. Where in the hell had she gone? She wasn't with Tucker, he was standing right next to him.

"Call her," Jace barked at Renie.

"What do you think I've been doing? I called her, I texted her. She isn't answering. And you can stop yelling at me now, Jace Rice."

"What's goin' on?" Billy put his arm around Renie's shoulder and scowled at Jace.

"Blythe left. We don't know where she is."

"Call her dad."

"You think she would've called him?" asked Jace.

Billy shook his head. "Why the hell would I tell you to call him if I didn't think so?"

Renie had her phone to her ear and was walking away. A couple minutes later, she came back, no longer on the phone.

"He said she's fine, but that's all he'd tell me."

"Where is she?"

"He wouldn't say, but he's coming to get her."

"How does he know for sure she's okay?"

"Jace!" Renie stamped her foot and put her hands on her hips. "Stop it. I told you what I know. *Her father* said she's okay, but that's all he'd say. Quit barking at me."

"Yep, this little lady right here, she's all mine," Billy bragged. "Spitfire, that's what she is. Damn that makes me hot, Renie. Let's get outta here."

Jace wanted to smack the smile off Billy Patterson's face. God damn smug bastard. He was worried sick about Blythe, and all Billy cared about was getting laid.

Renie slugged Billy for him but not as hard as he would've liked. Then she ruined it by smiling at him. She gave Jace a completely different look, one that would never be misconstrued as a smile.

"And you," she pointed at Tucker. "You started this. She was fine until you showed up."

Tucker raised his head and looked straight at her, but didn't say a word.

"Where's Lyric?" asked Jace.

"I have no idea," answered Renie. "Wasn't she here a minute ago?"

"Did they see you?" Blythe asked.

"I don't think so. They were too busy arguin'," Lyric answered.

"Thanks for rescuing me."

"No problem, girlfriend. Let's get outta here before they realize I'm gone and come lookin' for us."

Lyric was taking Blythe to meet up with some of her friends, ropers mainly. They weren't competing tonight and were hanging out at the Grizzly Rose bar, not far from the stock show.

"What about Renie, do you think you should at least let her know you're okay?"

"I did. She called and said she was pretending she was talking to my dad. She said she'd tell everybody I was okay and that's all she'd say."

"Shoulda figured."

"What?"

"You two. You don't even have to talk half the time, do ya? You're both so in sync with each other."

"It isn't always that way, or it hasn't been in the last year anyway."

"Let's go, girlfriend. Where we're headed the cowboys are gonna outnumber us ten to one. We'll be doin' a lot of dancin' tonight. Drinking too."

"I like you, Lyric. You're a good friend."

"Right back at ya, girl."

Jace stopped at the front desk to see if he could change his room from a king to one with two queens. It wasn't a problem.

He'd reserved a room near the National Western instead of staying with Billy and Renie, hoping Blythe would be sharing sheets with him. Now that Tuck was in town, that definitely wouldn't be happening.

He was stretched out on one of the beds when Tucker came in with a bottle of Crown Royal and a six-pack of cokes.

"Cups by the sink," Jace pointed.

"You get the ice?"

"Bucket's next to the cups."

"Coke?"

"Nah. Crown's good."

Tucker handed him the red solo cup. "Here's to Blythe," he said.

"Why'd you have to come back?"

"What'd you expect?"

"Why, Tuck? Why is she affecting us this way? *Shit.* I thought I was in love with Irene, and she didn't get under my skin this way."

"Yeah, she did."

"She did?"

"She's all you thought about when you were in Spain."

"So why Blythe?"

"I don't have an answer for you, bro. I feel the same way you do."

"I wanted to rip your face off when I saw you kissin' her."

"I know."

"Best thing would be for both of us to leave her alone."

"Not happenin'."

"You're not gonna give her up?"

"Nope."

"So it's up to me?"

"Yeah, it's up to you."

"She isn't gonna want to have anything to do with either one of us."

"Don't matter."

"I think you should come to work for me," Lyric said after their second shot with a beer chaser.

"What are you talking about?"

"For RodeoChat. It's growin' faster than I can keep up with. I need help."

Blythe laughed. "You want help from a girl who docsn't know shit about rodeo?"

"You don't seem to have any trouble attracting cowboys."

Blythe laughed. "We are having fun, aren't we?"

"Sure enough. But I'm not kidding. I need help. You can learn. I need someone who can help with interviews, make sure we're getting the scores as they happen—not only around the country, but also around the world. Most of the job will be research, and it's somethin' you'll have to be on top of, daily."

"You're serious?"

"Yeah, I'm serious. Dead serious."

"Where would I work?"

"You can work from home. You can work wherever you want."

"Where do you work?"

Lyric told her she spent most of her time traveling. "I've been thinking about moving to Colorado."

"Yeah?"

"Yep."

"I might have a place you can stay."

Blythe's parents had a rental house in Palmer Lake that had recently become vacant. She and her dad were supposed to get it ready for the next tenant. Maybe it was time for her to move out of her parents' house, and between the two of them, she and Lyric could probably swing the rent. Even if her parents offered it to them for free, Blythe wouldn't take them up on it. It was time she learned to live on her own, and make her own way.

"So what's the job pay anyway?"

The next night, Tucker was sitting in the box, waiting for the rodeo to start. Billy told him Liv and Ben would be here again tonight, and Renie was coming with them. No one expected Blythe to come along, so he was welcome to take her seat.

He'd just pulled out his sketchbook when the hair on the back of his neck stood up. He looked, and there she was, a couple of levels up, with the girl she and Renie had been with the night before. Interesting development.

Maybe Blythe's father hadn't come to get her at all. The girl had disappeared right after Blythe had gone missing, and no one saw her again. It was obvious what had happened.

He watched Blythe pull out a notepad while the other girl chatted up a couple of cowboys. The cowboys left, but the girl kept talking and Blythe kept writing. A minute later two more cowboys walked up, and the process began again.

"Do you know who that lady is?" he asked a guy sitting in the row behind him.

"Where?"

Tucker pointed.

"Yeah, that's Lyric Simmons. She hosts RodeoChat. She posted somethin' on Twitter earlier sayin' she be here tonight with her new sidekick. Guess that's her. That Lyric's got a good head on her shoulders."

Last night he and Jace had argued about Blythe but, eventually, came to an agreement. They'd both back off and let her make the next move. Neither would contact her, neither would pursue her. But now, seeing her, Tucker wondered if he'd be able to keep up his end of the deal.

He looked up again, and she was looking right at him. He tipped his hat, and she looked away.

"Did he see me?" she asked Lyric.

"Yep."

"Is he heading this way?"

"Nope. He's just sitting there. Looks like he went back to whatever he was doing before he saw you."

"Interesting. Maybe he got the message. I don't want anything to do with him or his brother."

"Careful what you wish for, I always say."

"What about you, Lyric? You think they're so hot, why don't you go after one of 'em?"

"Don't think that hasn't crossed my mind. I'm gonna wait and see how this thing with you plays out. Then...who knows? That Jace Rice is mighty fine. You'll get no argument from me about that."

"What about Tucker?"

"Girl, there isn't a woman with eyes who wouldn't see that Tucker's your man. You haven't figured it out yet, but he's it."

She laughed. Was it that obvious?

"What's so funny?"

"There's too much drama with Tucker. If you knew me better, you'd see the irony."

"I can only imagine. Okay, back to work. We have to figure out a way for me to interview Billy Patterson without you getting involved."

"Renie will be here later; she can set it up."

"Perfect. Now, let's make a game plan for the rest of the week."

Blythe got her laptop out and started posting day sheets from different rodeos around the country. As soon as results came in, she'd upload them.

Lyric had told her she didn't need to worry about her lack of rodeo knowledge and she'd been right. So far, it hadn't mattered. It would in the future, when Blythe was ready to take over some of the interviews, but until then, there was plenty she could do to help.

When the announcement came over the loudspeaker that the rodeo was about to begin, Blythe couldn't believe it. She'd been here two hours already, and it seemed more like two minutes.

"I love it already," she told Lyric as she set her laptop aside to stand for the national anthem.

"I can tell," Lyric whispered. "You're focused."

A few minutes later, Renie walked up with Willow, who was dressed like a little cowgirl. "I've been looking everywhere for you two."

"Is this Billy's daughter?" asked Lyric.

"This is *our* daughter, and her name is Willow," Renie answered.

"I'm sorry, I didn't mean anything by it, Renie."

"It's okay. Very few people know she isn't my biological daughter and we want to keep it that way. When she's old enough, we'll tell her about her mama, but until then, I'm the only mama she's got."

"I like that. You're a good mother, Renie."

"Thanks, Lyric. Won't be too long before Willow has a little brother or sister, will it, baby?"

"Wait, what?" Hadn't Renie said she was going back to school? Now she was pregnant?

"Calm down, Blythe," Renie laughed. "When I said, not too long, I meant a couple years from now."

"You damn near gave me a heart attack. Can you Fairchild women slow down with the breeding, please?"

"What's she talkin' about?" asked Lyric.

"My mom and Ben are having a baby."

"They are?"

"She's not that old, Lyric. She's forty-one. I can assure you, there are many women her age having babies."

"But she'll be in her sixties by the time the kid graduates from high school."

"You two are meant for each other." Renie shook her head. "Neither one of you has a filter."

"What do you mean?" asked Lyric.

"Ask Blythe to explain it to you," she heard Renie suggest, but Blythe wasn't paying close attention to them. "I've never seen her so focused, and I've known her since we were five."

"I think she likes her new job."

Blythe heard that part, and Lyric was right. She felt as though she'd finally found the thing she was supposed to do, and she'd just gotten started.

"Shouldn't tell ya this," Billy said to Jace who was getting ready to head to the chutes.

"Yeah? But you're gonna anyway?"

"Blythe's here."

Jace scowled. "You shouldn't have told me, Billy."

"God, who am I? I don't even know why I did." Billy scratched his head. "I saw her a couple hours ago, and I wasn't gonna tell you, but you rode pretty damn good last night. Thought it might help to know she's watchin'."

Would it? Did his ride last night have anything to do with her, or was he determined to do the best he could tonight because he was so pissed off at her and Tucker?

He looked over to see if his brother was still in the box. He was, and it looked like he was sketching. Probably Blythe, but at least he hadn't gone chasing after her.

"Ready?" Billy asked.

"As I'll ever be." He lowered himself on the bronc he'd drawn for tonight's ride, got himself as settled as he could on an animal who couldn't wait to get him the hell off his back, and nodded to the guys pulling the chute open that he was ready.

Eight seconds later, Jace finished another good ride. His scores were low, but at least he didn't buck off.

Billy rode great a few minutes later, and was still sitting in first place at the end of the night.

"I can't believe you're gonna retire," Jace said when they were putting away their gear.

"It's time. Not gettin' any younger."

"You could've ridden the bronc you drew tonight, in your sleep."

Billy shook his head.

"Is Irene pressuring you to quit?"

Billy stopped what he was doing and turned to face Jace. "If you think she'd do that, then you don't know her at all."

Yeah, he thought, that really didn't sound like her. Or like Billy. If he was retiring, it was his decision and no one else's.

"We're goin' to the Grizzly Rose after. Wanna come?"

Blythe shot Lyric a glare when she heard her invite Renie out with them.

"I don't think Blythe wants me to go," laughed Renie.

"It isn't that. If you go, so will Billy, and then Jace and Tucker will come along, and…"

"Tucker said they're backing off."

"He told you that?"

"Yep," Renie confirmed. "In fact, he told me to tell you so if I saw you."

Interesting. Well, she did disappear last night. As Lyric said, be careful what you wish for.

"Well, then, sure. Come along with us. If they're gonna leave me alone, then I don't care whether they come or not."

Renie and Lyric both raised their eyebrows.

"I'm serious. They're too much drama."

Renie burst out laughing.

"Shut up," Blythe muttered. "You've gotten to be worse than me."

"No," Renie spit out between giggles. "No one will ever be more dramatic than you, Blythe."

"I thought the whole point was to stay away from her."

"It was, sort of. I mean, if we're where she is and don't ask her to dance, or if neither one of us is workin' hard to get in her panties, she'll realize *faster* that we're backin' off," Jace told Tucker.

"I don't know. I'm having a pretty hard time not thinkin' about her panties. It might be more than I can handle, watchin' her dance. What if some cowboy comes on a little too strong? You're not gonna be tempted to stop him?"

"Would you rather be there to save her from someone like that, or be at the hotel wonderin' what the hell she's up to for the second night in a row."

"I'm gonna punt. You have fun."

"Seriously? You're tellin' me to go, and you're not gonna? I can't believe it."

"Fuck off."

"You're goin', aren't ya?"

"Of course I am, asshole."

In the end, it didn't matter what they did.

Blythe was line-dancing when she saw Renie, who was sitting at a nearby high-top table, look at her phone. Eyes wide, Renie's face drained of all color. Blythe stopped dancing, stopped moving at all, as everything around her shifted into slow motion.

Renie stood and sought her in the crowd. When her best friend's eyes filled with tears, Blythe took a step backward, and then another. She kept moving backward until she felt a hard body behind her. Strong hands rested on her shoulders and squeezed.

"Renie's gonna drive you home, darlin'. Lyric's goin' with you." Billy's voice was quiet and soothing in a bar where loud music reverberated from gigantic speakers lining the dance floor. It was as though his words had been mixed out of the background, and the volume increased so she could hear him as clearly as if they were standing in an empty, silent room.

"What happened?"

"Let's go outside." Lyric pulled her toward the back door of the club; Renie and Billy followed.

Blythe started to shake, unsure whether it was because of the frigid winter wind, or if it was her body's reaction to hearing the bad news she knew was coming.

Billy covered her bare shoulders with his heavy barn jacket. Her eyes met Renie's and she waited for her friend to find the words to tell her what happened.

"It's your dad," Renie said, handing her the phone.

8

Blythe listened to her father's words, trying to process what he was telling her.

There had been an accident, he told her. They were waiting for word, but the news coming out of Afghanistan wasn't good. Her sister Bree's husband was reported dead after an IED hit the truck he was riding in.

Where is Bree? The same three words repeated over and over in her head, like song lyrics. She couldn't remember where her sister was, and when she asked, Renie said she wasn't sure.

"My mom is on her way to your parents' house," Renie told her.

Blythe nodded. If anyone knew how to counsel their family, it was Liv. Her first husband had been killed in the Gulf War shortly after they were married, before Renie was born.

When Blythe walked into the kitchen of her parents' house, her mother was on the phone. Whenever there was a crisis, Paige Cochran took over. It didn't matter what it was, the first words out of her mom's mouth were always, "What can I do?" This time the crisis was in her own family, but her mom still went into management mode.

Paige put her hand over the receiver. "I'm talking to Zack's parents. Your dad is talking to someone with the Air Force. We'll know more in a minute."

Her dad was able to confirm that Zack had been killed during a combat advisory mission with Afghan National Army Commandos, and that a car bomb had detonated near his convoy.

All they knew now was that Zack's body would be repatriated back to the United States as soon as possible. What they were hearing was that he'd be flown to Dover, in Delaware, but they had no idea when.

"What can I do?" Blythe asked.

"Bree will need your support when she gets here. Or when we go there; we don't know what she wants to do yet."

"Can I talk to her?"

"Of course you can, baby. Call her."

Blythe went upstairs to make the call. Renie went with her and sat on the edge of the bed.

"I just want everyone to leave," her sister said, explaining that soon after the commander of the base came to the door, asked if he could come in, and told her the horrible news, women she barely knew surrounded her.

"Who are they?"

"Air Force wives, and I don't want them here."

"I think it's better if you have someone with you."

"I don't even know them. They're making me uncomfortable."

Bree and Zack had only been at the base a couple of months before he was deployed. She'd met several people, as was customary as an Air Force officer's wife, but—as she told Blythe when they talked at Christmas—she hadn't gotten to know any of them well.

"I'll be there tomorrow," Blythe said, not knowing how she'd manage it, but she would.

"What do you mean?"

"I'm flying out first thing in the morning. I'll be there before noon."

Renie had stepped out of the room and met Blythe on her way down the stairs.

"I'll take you to the airport tomorrow morning," Renie told her. "We'll meet Ben there, and he and his dad will fly you to California." Ben and his father were both pilots and owned a plane they shared.

"That's a lot to ask."

"Blythe, let them do this."

Traveling by private plane meant the journey from Centennial airport to the one in Sacramento, which would've taken her all day if she'd taken a commercial flight, took only a little over two hours.

Shortly after they landed, Ben rented a car and drove Blythe to her sister's house on the base.

The next few days were a blur. Bree slept intermittently, and when she did, she had nightmares. Blythe slept with her so she'd be there when the bad dreams woke her sister.

The Air Force made arrangements to fly Bree to Dover, and Blythe went with her. After they arrived, they sat at the airport for several more hours, waiting for word on when the plane carrying Zach's body would arrive.

"I'm so sorry," she told Lyric when she had a minute to check in with her new boss.

"Please, don't be sorry. You have to do this, and I understand."

"But you just hired me." Blythe figured this would be another in a long list of jobs she lost.

"Blythe, listen to me. I need your help, but I don't need it this week. Your sister does."

"I'm sorry," Blythe said again, her voice cracking. "I can't stop crying. Thank you, Lyric."

"I'm here if you need me, Blythe. I'm not your boss, I'm your friend. That comes first. Let me know what I can do, and I'll do it." Renie had said the same thing.

"I have to go," she told Lyric when she saw a uniformed man approaching her sister.

"The plane is making its final descent," she heard him say. "Please, follow me."

"Who are all these other people?" Blythe asked the officer as they escorted Bree out of the building and to the tarmac, when she saw a crowd of people.

"The Dignified Arrival team, ma'am," he answered as though Blythe would know what that meant.

"Protocol," he added.

"What can we do?" Jace called Renie and asked.

"I don't know. Nothing right now."

"How is she?"

"Okay, more worried about her sister, of course. They'll be back in Colorado tomorrow morning."

"Tucker and I would like to attend the services, but we don't want to intrude."

"I'm sure it would mean a lot to her if you were there, Jace."

"What did she say?" Tucker asked when Jace hung up.

"She'll let us know."

"This can't be a game anymore."

"It never has been to me, Tucker."

"Me, neither."

"I can't believe I'm saying this, but…" Jace couldn't bring himself to finish his sentence. Here he was, giving up again. First Renie, now Blythe.

"I wish I could be the bigger man here, but I can't. I think I love her. I know that sounds crazy, but there hasn't been anyone I've felt this way about since—"

"I know," Jace stopped him. He owed his brother, and even though Tucker would never know the real reason he was giving up on Blythe, Jace would assuage part of the guilt he'd been carrying around with him these last few years.

He rubbed his chest, the place where it felt like a ton of bricks sat.

Three days later, Blythe and Bree boarded the plane that would carry Zack's body to Peterson Air Force base in Colorado Springs, where the funeral would take place.

They spent the night at their parents' house, and the next morning, rode in the car with them, while Zack's family followed behind them. Several other vehicles were in the procession, but Blythe had no idea who was in them.

They waited at the front gate, for their escort to the tarmac.

"*No!*" Bree gasped when the military personnel directed them where to park.

"What, honey? What's wrong?" asked Paige.

"No hearses. *I said no.*"

Paige looked at Blythe, who shrugged her shoulders.

Mark put his hand on Bree's. "Honey, tell us what you're talking about."

"I said no hearses."

"I'll take care of it," said their mother.

The military escort led Bree and Mark into a building and upstairs, to a waiting area, while Paige and Blythe went in search of someone who might be able to explain what Bree was upset about.

"May I help you, ma'am?" another gentleman in uniform asked.

"I'm Paige Cochran, my daughter—"

"Yes, ma'am," he interrupted and put his hand on hers. "I'm Colonel Stevens. I was Zack's commanding officer. You're Bree's mother. What can I help you with?"

"Bree saw the hearse on the tarmac and was very upset by it. She kept insisting she'd said no. I don't know what she meant. Do you?"

"Yes, ma'am. I do. And it's being taken care of."

"Can you please explain it to me so I understand?"

"Bree requested that Zack's body not be transported by hearse. Her words were, 'he's too young for a hearse, no hearses.' We made arrangements for a Humvee transport instead. Again, at her request."

"I see," her mother answered, her eyes filling with tears.

When they walked back into the waiting room, Blythe saw Bree sitting in a smaller side room with their dad. He met them outside the door he'd closed behind him.

"She wants to be alone," he told them.

"What do you mean?"

"Bree asked to be left alone. Just Blythe."

"Bree asked to be left alone. Just Blythe."

Paige nodded and motioned for Blythe to go in. Zack's mom and dad were also in the room, but no one spoke.

A few minutes later, the colonel she and her mom had talked with, came in the room, and spoke with Zack's parents.

Zack's mother put her hand in her husband's when he turned away. He turned back, but he did not speak.

"There has been a delay," they overheard the colonel explain. "The plane should be arriving in approximately one hour. I will keep you informed as I receive further information."

Colonel Stevens left and returned again, before the end of the hour, to let them know there was another delay. The plane had not yet left Dover. This delay would be several hours.

"I'll tell Mom and Dad," Blythe said to Bree, who only nodded.

"How is she?" Paige asked.

"Gone. Completely shut down."

"I'm glad you're with her."

"Don't be upset, Mom."

"Oh, honey, I'm not. I meant what I said. I'm glad she has you to lean on."

"When will Brooke and Tom be here?" Her older sister and her husband were in Germany, where he was stationed at the Air Force base in Ramstein. She knew, without having to be told, that the Air Force would transport them here for Zack's funeral.

"This afternoon. I told her I'd let her know where we were when they landed. Has Bree asked?"

"No, but we all need to be together, Mom."

The colonel offered to take people to another building to get something to eat, but Blythe knew her sister wouldn't want to go.

"I'll stay here with Bree, but you and Dad should go."

"Do you want us to bring something back?" Paige offered.

"I'm not hungry, Mom. I'm sure Bree isn't either."

"I'll bring it anyway. You don't have to eat if you're still not hungry."

"Thanks, Mom." Blythe turned to go back in the room where Bree waited.

"Honey, did you want to say hello to Tucker? He's been here since this morning."

"Why? Where is he?" she asked her mother, her voice almost a whisper.

Paige pointed to where Renie stood with Billy. Tucker was with them.

She wanted to walk to him, but she couldn't move. She needed all of her strength, all of her energy, to take care of her sister. If she talked to Tucker or anyone else, she'd fall apart.

Finally word came that the plane was less than an hour away. The protocol staff briefed them on what would be happening. Only immediate family would be allowed on the tarmac when the plane landed. Other friends and family would be escorted into the viewing room where Blythe and Bree had spent the afternoon waiting with Zack's parents.

Blythe held Bree's hand as they walked outside—the scene, so much like what they'd just experienced in Dover except, this time, both their parents and Zack's were with them.

The colonel approached to escort Bree and Zack's parents closer. Blythe, her mom and dad, and Zack's brother waited behind them. The color guard and armed guards marched onto the tarmac and approached the plane where it had come to a stop. The door opened, and the casket, draped in the American flag, was carried down by more men in uniform.

Blythe saw Bree about to fall before anyone else did, and moved closer. "Lean on me," she whispered, trying hard not to cry herself. Bree's sobs were almost more than she could bear.

When Zack's casket was moved in front of them, near the rear door of the Humvee, Bree's sobs grew louder. It was the worst sound Blythe had ever heard. Zack's father leaned forward and put his hand on the casket. His mother buried her head on her husband's chest.

Blythe squeezed her sister's hand, and then let go. When Zack's parents stepped away, Bree walked forward and laid her hands on the top of the casket and cried.

The military personnel waited, but it soon became evident that Bree would not leave the casket. When approached, Bree shook her head and climbed into the Humvee after they loaded the casket in, and rode to the funeral home alongside her husband.

As the cars in the processional left the tarmac and drove toward the gates of Peterson Air Force Base, every surface street was lined with soldiers, standing at attention and saluting as the Humvee passed. There were hundreds.

As they drove through the streets of Colorado Springs, cars were pulled off to the side of the road. As they passed, Blythe saw many of the drivers had gotten out of their cars and were saluting, too.

Colorado Springs was home to Peterson Air Force Base, Schriever Air Force Base, Fort Carson Army installation, and the Air Force Academy. Heartbreaking as it was to think about, military funerals took place too often in this community that was also home to many who had retired from active duty.

When they arrived at the funeral home, Blythe got out of the car and went to look for Bree. She found her sitting in a room, alone with the casket.

"What can I do?" Blythe whispered.

"Bring him back," she answered.

More than four thousand people attended the visitation the next day. It started at two in the afternoon and did not end until nine that evening. Many who came, laid military coins or patches in the open casket.

As a former Air Force Academy cadet and graduate of the prestigious institution, there were countless stories about his willingness to serve his country, his loyalty, his sense of humor, and his goodness.

Blythe hadn't realized that he'd volunteered for the Afghan deployment until she overheard someone talking to Bree about it. Even more tragic, that deployment was scheduled to end less than thirty days after he was killed.

Blythe saw Tucker, standing not too far away, and walked over to him.

"You're here."

"Yes, I am."

"Why?"

"Because I care about you."

"But you haven't talked to me."

"No, but I've been nearby. If you needed me, I was close."

He opened his arms and Blythe buried her head in his comfort. "I need you now," she cried. "Tomorrow is the funeral."

"I know, sweetheart."

"Will you be there?"

"I will be."

"Will you sit near me?"

He pulled her into a hallway where they were alone. "Of course, I will."

She let herself cry harder, knowing no one could see her. "I'm sorry," she said, pulling back.

"You've been so strong for your sister. She'd be lost without you."

"Do you think so?"

"I know so. I'm so proud of you, Blythe."

She let more of the tears fall that she'd struggled to hold inside. The stress of the last few days was wearing on her. She had no idea whether she was doing the right things for Bree, but Tucker said she was, and that made her feel better.

The service at the church was standing-room only, in a building that held five thousand people. Blythe sat in the row behind her sister and parents, with her older sister, Brooke, and her husband. Several times, she reached out and put her hand on her sister's shoulder, and Bree covered Blythe's with her own.

The casket, surrounded by the color guard, followed the single bagpiper down the aisle. As it passed, airmen raised sabers, one by one.

After the pastor spoke, scriptures were read, Zack's commander spoke, and one of Zack's childhood friends read a poem written by his mother. The stanzas connected his deep reverence for the natural world with reminders that he was on the right path in his life and faith, and urged people not to weep for him because of his sacrifice.

Mark was asked to sing, and when he did, Blythe thought it was the most beautiful thing she'd ever heard. Her father's voice always brought her to tears, but this time, it was different. Usually she cried tears of joy when he sang. Today it was about sacrifice and tragedy.

Every time people said Zack was with God now, or he was a hero for serving his country, all Blythe could think was that he'd left his wife, the woman he'd loved—the woman who loved him. Heroism didn't matter, love did.

Blythe had no more tears to shed. She wanted to go home and hide in her room, away from everyone, but she couldn't. Bree needed her. Even though Brooke was there, Blythe was the sister Bree turned to.

She raised her head and looked two rows behind her, where Tucker and Jace sat.

Tucker's eyes were red; he'd been crying, too. She wanted to look at Jace, to acknowledge his presence, but she couldn't look away from Tucker. She wished he could've sat with her, held her hand, given her his comfort. Moments earlier, she'd wanted to leave alone, not see anyone for days. Now she didn't want to be alone. She wanted to be with Tucker. She wanted him to take her away, comfort her, and tell her all of this was a bad dream.

Blythe couldn't take her eyes from Tucker's, but when her mother touched her arm, she turned around.

"When will it be over?" she whispered.

"Soon," Paige answered.

The colonel who had been with the family when the casket landed at Peterson, and at the visitation the day before, came forward and began a roll call of Zack's squadron. When their names were called, each soldier in attendance answered. Then the colonel called Zack's name.

"Captain Fox?" There was no response.

"Captain Zackary Fox?"

"Captain Zackary Jonathan Fox?"

That was Zack's final roll call. His name called three times and left unanswered meant he had left his unit.

The casket was being transported to the cemetery by Humvee, also per Bree's request, but this time she agreed to ride in the limousine with her family. Blythe kept her arm around her sister as they walked to the car.

When she stumbled, Blythe could not catch her quickly enough. Before she realized what was happening, Tucker was there, helping her hold her sister up, getting her to the car.

"Thank you," Blythe whispered.

"Of course," Tucker answered.

Blythe climbed in with Bree and closed the door. Her sister fell against her and cried even harder than she had been.

Shock was the body's defense against the pain it knew it wasn't capable of handling. When it wore off, there would be no choice for her but to work her way through her grief. Blythe never wanted to feel the things Bree was experiencing, but how did she avoid it? If she loved, there was always the possibility of loss.

She and Bree had talked about it on the flight from Dover, home. Would she have chosen not to be with Zack had she known this would happen? If she'd known she'd lose him so young, so tragically, would she still have let herself fall in love with him? Would she still have married him?

Yes, Bree told her. She'd do it all again. She'd loved Zack and wouldn't trade any of her time with him even if it meant she could avoid the pain she was in now.

Blythe doubted she could be as brave as her sister was.

Paige and Mark joined their daughters in the limo. Paige took Bree in her arms and Mark comforted Blythe. She'd never been so thankful for her parents. She'd done her best to be strong for her sister, but she needed comfort herself. Did that make her weak?

Blythe pulled away from her dad.

"What?"

"Bree needs you," she said softly.

"So do you," he answered, pulling her back into him. "It's okay, sweetheart. You can let go."

Blythe buried her face in her father's shoulder and let herself cry.

At the cemetery on the Air Force Academy grounds, Zack's brother read the list of the awards his brother was being given posthumously—the Bronze Star, Meritorious Service Medal, Purple Heart, and the Air Force Combat Action Medal. Again, to Blythe, none of that mattered. Every time she looked at her sister, she saw a broken heart no award would mend.

After they lowered the casket into the ground, the minister asked that the family be given some privacy, and the crowd dispersed respectfully.

Blythe saw Liv and Renie walking to another part of the cemetery. She had forgotten that Renie's father was buried here, too.

9

Zack's family came back to her parents' house, and several of Bree and Zack's friends came, too. As they were leaving the cemetery, Renie asked if she wanted them to come to the house, but Blythe told her it would be okay if they didn't. Blythe wanted to escape for a little while, if only to her bedroom. If Renie and Billy came to the house, she'd feel as though she'd have to talk to them.

"Take me for a drive?" she said to Tucker when he walked in the front door.

He didn't answer but put his jacket back on and turned around.

"I'll tell my mom—"

He nodded his head and slipped out the door before she finished her sentence.

Tucker needed a few minutes to himself. He doubted he'd have that long, but he'd take whatever time he could get. He'd never wanted to bury himself in a woman more than he wanted to right now. And not only for her comfort, for his, too.

Grief was palpable, and it had surrounded both of them the last few days. Witnessing it had brought it all back to him. It hadn't been her pain alone he experienced. He relived his own pain—it engulfed him.

He wanted to feel something else, anything. All he could think about was running his hands over Blythe's body, nuzzling himself into her, and holding her nakedness next to his own.

She said she wanted to go for a drive. He hoped she knew where she wanted to go. He'd been staying at the inn in Palmer Lake, and right now, it was the only place he could think to take her.

Blythe opened the door and slid onto the seat next to him, and brought her mouth to his. "I need you, Tucker," she whispered.

The first time she and Tucker kissed, it had been slow and languid. This kiss was nothing like that. It was hot and hard. It took her breath away and made her want to climb on top of him right there, in her parents' driveway.

He pulled away first.

"Blythe, honey, stop for a minute."

She froze. What was she doing? Her sister's husband had just died. What must he think of her? She lunged for the passenger door.

"Wait," he said, grabbing her arm. "Where are you going?"

"It's okay. If you don't want this—"

"Hold on." He pulled her back inside. "I didn't say that." He took a deep breath. "There isn't anything I want more."

"Why did you stop, then?"

"Let's get something straight right now. It isn't because I don't want you."

She watched his mouth as he spoke. She wanted him to stop talking and kiss her instead.

"You gotta stop looking at me like that."

She closed her eyes. If he didn't have an iron grip on her, she'd try to scoot away again. She shifted to see if he would let her go.

"Blythe. Please. Stop moving, baby. Sit still for a minute. I'm trying to talk to you."

"Since when do you want to talk?"

Tucker started the truck but kept his arm wrapped around her shoulder.

"What are you doing?"

He didn't answer. If she didn't want him to talk, he wouldn't.

"Tucker?"

He stopped at the end of the block, pulled the truck over, and kissed her again.

Couldn't she feel the heat between them? How could she think he didn't want her? But he didn't want it like this. He wanted them to connect, to comfort each other. When his body touched hers, he wanted to know their souls were touching, too.

He put the truck back in gear.

"Are you going to tell me where you're taking me?"

He didn't answer.

She crossed her arms in front of her. Didn't she know what it did to her breasts when she did that?

He pulled around to the back door of the inn and parked the truck.

"Look at me," he said. "Is this what you want, Blythe? Because, if it isn't, you need to tell me now. If we do this, everything changes. Everything."

Was she ready? Part of her had been ready the first time he kissed her, on the porch of Ben Rice's house in Crested Butte. When he'd slid his hand up and cupped her breast, she'd wanted him to make love to her there and then. And later that night, on their way home from dinner, when Tucker had stopped the truck and kissed her. She'd been ready then, too.

"Blythe, answer me."

She looked into his eyes. Yes, she was ready. She told herself Tucker and Jace confused her, that she didn't know which of the Rice twins she wanted, but the truth was, she'd known all along. Even when they'd met and she looked into his brooding eyes, she'd known then she wanted him and no one else.

"I want this, Tucker," she breathed.

His hand gripped her neck as his lips covered hers, taking possession of her mouth. His other hand slid up under her shirt and caressed her skin.

"Let's go inside." He wanted every part of her body touching his. Even when they got to the door of his room, he didn't want to let her go. His heart pounded as adrenaline surged through his veins. He couldn't breathe with wanting her.

He wouldn't let go of her until he could lay his body on hers. His shoulder hit the light switch when he opened the door, and they walked inside the room.

She climbed on the bed and lay on her back. Tucker rested his elbows on either side of her. He wasn't gentle or easy when he pressed his hard body onto hers. He took possession of her mouth in the same way he planned to take possession of her body, as soon as he could.

She turned her face to the side, and he saw her tears.

"Sweetheart…" He rolled so they were side by side, and held her while she cried. "Get it out, baby. Cry as long as you need to. I've got you."

Blythe had tried so hard to hold it in, keep it from her sister and her family, but now it poured out of her. Once she started crying, she couldn't stop.

"I want more, Tucker." She wanted his hands on her. She pulled back and rolled so she was straddling his body, and rested her hands on his chest.

Tucker put his hands on her waist, pushing up her shirt as he did. Blythe grabbed the hem and pulled it off. He nuzzled his head between her breasts, wrapped his arms around her waist, and unfastened her bra. He pulled it away as she shimmied her arms from it. When his cheek met her skin, she shuddered. When his mouth replaced his cheek, she cried out.

He rolled again, so she was back under him. With one hand, he unzipped her pants. She helped slide them down over her hips then her legs then her feet.

Tucker caressed her bare hip, shifted to his side, and gazed at her nakedness. His lips followed the path his hands ran over her body.

She was in agony. As much as she knew he would take his time, she didn't want him to. Blythe grabbed at his jeans, trying to unzip them, urging him to be as naked as she was.

He let go of her and stood. "Be right back."

"Wait. Where are you going?"

Tucker rummaged through his shaving kit. She watched as he closed his eyes and looked up at the ceiling.

"Blythe, honey. God, I'm so sorry. I don't have any condoms."

"It's okay; I'm on the pill."

"I haven't—"

"Tucker, I don't want to talk. Please, get the rest of your clothes off. *Now.*"

She closed her eyes, praying he would listen to her. When she opened them, his clothes were off and he was kneeling next to her. He pushed his way between her legs and came down on top of her, resting his arms on either side of her. He pulled her as close as he could and slid inside her.

She took possession of his mouth in the same way he had hers. He began to move, and before she could catch her breath, they both cried out together.

When Jace got to the house, he looked for Blythe and Tucker, but couldn't find either of them. He peeked his head into the music room.

"They left," someone said.

The voice, coming from the dark and quiet room, startled him.

"I'm sorry I disturbed you."

He thought he heard a laugh, but he quickly realized it was sobbing instead. It had to be Bree, but it was too dark for him to be sure.

"Can I do anything for you?"

"Everyone keeps asking me that. There's only one thing anyone can do."

"What's that, sweetheart?" he asked.

"Bring him back to me."

Blythe and Tucker made love all night, over and over again—both insatiable. When the sun rose, they slept. Later, he woke her again with his mouth, and they began the dance again.

"Do you need anything?" he whispered when they both were, once again, sated.

"I'm hungry."

Tucker didn't have to move very far to reach the menu where it sat on the nightstand. "What looks good?"

"You decide."

He smiled down at her. He'd guessed that first time they'd had dinner that Blythe liked when he decided for her. A lot, in fact. He pressed the button on the room phone and ordered.

He was still on top of her, resting most of his weight on her body. He had to be hurting her, but she showed no sign of it. She shifted so he rested between her legs. She reached down and put him inside her. She didn't seem to care that he was still on the phone as she began to move beneath him. It was all he could do to hang up rather than let the phone fall to the floor.

"I should check in," she said later.

"Who with?"

"I didn't tell my mom where we were going."

"I texted Renie. She let your mom know."

"How did you get Renie's number?"

"I used your phone."

"Why didn't you text my mom?"

"I told Renie it was me and asked her to let everyone know you were here with me. It would've been a much different conversation with your mother, even if it was only a text."

"Oh."

Tucker figured things out and took care of what needed to be taken care of. He made decisions, and he acted on them. Shouldn't she appreciate that about him and not make a big deal about the fact that he used her phone and messaged someone? With his lips on her neck, slowly making their way down her body, she decided not to question a damn thing Tucker did. At least not right now.

Jace was in the kitchen, having coffee with Paige, wondering where Tucker and Blythe were. He knew she was with him; he just didn't know where.

"She's with your brother, and it's the best place for her right now."

He nodded, wishing she wasn't right. "I know Tucker will take care of her."

"Jace, do you know my oldest daughter, Brooke?"

Jace stood to shake the hand of the woman who had stalked into the kitchen.

"Where did you say Blythe is?" Brooke stood with her hands on her hips, ignoring Jace and glaring at her mother.

"She's with Jace's brother, Tucker."

"Did she spend the night with him?"

"Brooke, Blythe is a grown woman, who shouldered more than her share of responsibility over the course of the last several days. Let it go. It's none of your business."

Mark walked into the kitchen as Brooke stormed out.

"What's wrong with her?" he asked.

"She asked where Blythe was, and when I told her it was none of her business, she stormed out." Paige turned to Jace. "Sorry, she's not our most sociable daughter. I need some fresh air." Paige went out on the deck and closed the door behind her.

Maybe coming over here this morning hadn't been Jace's best idea, especially since Bree came in and sat at the dining room table, next to him.

"Where did you say Blythe is?" she asked.

"Out with some guy," Brooke answered from the other room. "Overnight, I might add." She came back into the kitchen and stood next to Bree's chair.

Bree stood and tried to get past her sister, who blocked her from leaving.

"For Christ's sake, Brooke, why the hell don't you go back to Germany?"

Brooke looked from Bree to her father, expecting him to defend her. He only raised an eyebrow. Jace wanted to excuse himself, but in order to do so, he'd have to walk between the sisters whose argument was becoming increasingly heated.

"She isn't a little girl anymore, you know," Bree went on, glaring at Brooke. "She doesn't have to ask permission to stay out all night. Especially from you."

"So you're okay with her acting like a slut?"

Jace watched the tension travel up Bree's spine, into her arms, up her neck, until it settled in bright red splotches on her face. He saw her bring her hand back, and before he could stop her, Bree slapped her sister across the face. The crack of her palm meeting her sister's cheek resounded through the kitchen, and the force behind it shook the coffee cups hanging near the coffee maker.

Brooke stood motionless with her hand on her cheek, looking at her father.

"I think you should leave, Brooke," he said.

"But, Dad—"

"*Brooke!*" he shouted. "*Leave.*"

Brooke stormed out of the kitchen, the same way she had a few minutes earlier.

"I won't apologize to her, Daddy."

"I don't expect you to."

"She's a condescending bitch."

"She can be that."

"I'm not putting up with anybody's shit."

"You could say we picked up on that already, Bree."

Jace stood to make his exit, hoping no one would notice.

"Where are you going?" Bree challenged him.

Jace looked around the kitchen, hoping she was talking to anyone but him.

Mark put his hand on Jace's shoulder. "You don't have sisters, do you?"

Jace shook his head, cursing himself again for coming over here this morning. "No, sir," he answered.

"Drama has been a steady part of my life for thirty years. I forget not everyone is used to it. Can I get you anything?"

"I'd love a Bloody Mary," Bree answered before Jace could.

"You got it. How about you, Jace?"

"Sounds good. Thanks." A little alcohol might help ease the tension that had engulfed the room, and him along with it. "What can I do to help?"

Mark pointed Jace in the direction of the liquor cabinet while he pulled ingredients from the pantry.

"We like to make our own," Mark explained, waving his hand over the full counter. "Mix your own poison."

By the time Paige came back inside, Bree was almost finished with her first drink, and Mark was in the midst of laying out a breakfast buffet.

"How are you this morning, baby?" she asked Bree.

"Better now that she took out some of her anger on her older sister," Mark answered.

"What happened?"

"I slapped her."

Paige looked at Mark.

"She deserved it."

Paige got up to look for Brooke, but Bree put her hand on her mother's arm. "Stay, Mom. Please," she said softly.

Paige sat back down, and Jace downed the contents of his first drink of the day. Something told him there'd be more.

"I should ask you to take me home."

"Why?" Tucker had no intention of taking her home, whether she asked or not. He needed her with him, and whether she realized it or not, she needed him.

"I don't know, for Bree mainly. I feel as though I deserted her."

"She has the rest of your family with her. She'll be okay. You were there for the hardest part."

"But my older sister can be...kind of a bitch. Maybe I should at least call and see how's she's doing."

"If it makes you feel better."

Blythe opened the sliding glass door and went out on the patio. She intended to call home, but she called Renie instead.

"I'm with Tucker."

"I heard."

"What do you mean?"

"He texted me. Didn't he tell you?"

"Oh yeah, he did."

"I guess Bree and Brooke got into a fist fight over it."

"*What?*"

"Sorry, I was joking. It wasn't quite that bad. But your mom told my mom that Bree slapped her."

"She slapped Brooke?"

"Yeah."

That made them both laugh. If there was anyone who deserved to be slapped every now and then, it was Brooke.

"Wait, which part were you joking about? Did Bree slap Brooke over something to do with me?"

"She did. I guess Brooke was making a fuss about you being out all night, and both Bree and your mom told her to mind her own business."

Blythe had never gotten along with her oldest sister. Brooke married the first guy she ever had sex with, and she was pretty sure they'd waited until after they were married. There wasn't anything wrong with living your life that way, until you started to preach to everyone else about it. That was the part Blythe didn't like. Bree didn't either.

Blythe thought Brooke walked around with a stick up her ass, but she didn't try to tell her to live her life any differently. She couldn't believe that, only a couple of days ago, she told her mom she wished Brooke was there.

"How's Bree?"

"She's okay. She's spending time with your mom and dad. You're okay, Blythe. Take some time for yourself. She'll be fine."

Blythe went back inside without calling home. No one had called or texted, and if they'd needed her, someone would've. Renie was right, she'd take some time for herself and not feel guilty about it.

"Everything okay?"

"I'm not sure. But...nobody needs me. So..."

"Wrong. I need you. Come over here, Blythe."

Tucker was stretched out on the bed. The same bed they'd barely gotten out of since they got to the room last night.

"Wanna go for a walk or something?" she asked.

"Nope."

"You wanna stay in bed all day?"

"Yep."

Who was she to argue? Blythe took off the robe she'd found on the back of the bathroom door, and stretched out on the bed next to him.

10

"We should talk, Blythe."

She didn't want to talk. She'd done nothing but talk and listen for the last week. What was wrong with feeling? The last few hours with Tucker had been all about feeling. She buried her head under a pillow.

"I take it you don't want to talk."

She threw the pillow on the floor. "Why do we have to talk?" she pouted. Whenever someone said they needed to talk, it usually meant they had something to tell her that she didn't want to hear. Otherwise, they just talked. They didn't announce the need for it.

Tucker smiled. Even if he didn't know, he'd be able to guess that Blythe was the baby of the family, and her daddy's little girl. She was a lot like her dad, so it made sense.

"It's time for me to go back to Aspen."

Blythe got up, went into the bathroom, and closed the door. When she came back out, she was dressed.

"Can you take me home now?"

"No."

"You're refusing?" She went to pick her phone up from the nightstand, but he grabbed it first.

"I told you I wanted to talk. Let's talk first, and then I'll take you home."

"I want to go home."

"Why?"

She sat down on the end of the bed, with her back to him.

"I don't understand why you're getting upset about something as simple as me saying we should talk."

"Why did you leave on Thanksgiving?"

"It's a long story."

Blythe kept her back to him. "Since you're refusing to take me home, I have all the time in the world."

"Now isn't the time for us to talk about that."

"You say you want to talk, yet you aren't willing to."

"I don't want to get into what happened on Thanksgiving right now. That's it."

"Oh yeah? What about your scar, Tucker?" Blythe turned to face him and ran her finger along the thin line that went from his left cheek almost all the way to his hairline.

"Same story, Blythe."

"Fine," she turned back around. "Then, take me home."

He stood, so she did too, assuming they were leaving.

"I'm not playing games with you, Blythe."

"Good, because I'm not playing games either. Take me home, or I'll call someone to come and get me."

Tucker put his hands on her shoulders. "Blythe, why are you acting this way? All I said was it was time for me to go home. I didn't say I didn't want to see you again."

Why was she acting this way? Good question, and one she didn't have a rational answer for. The minute he'd said he was leaving, she wanted to leave first.

She sat back down, and he sat next to her. "Blythe, what's goin' on?"

He put his arm around her shoulder and drew her back, so they were stretched out on the bed, side by side. Turning to face her, Tucker put his hand under her shirt and caressed the skin on her stomach.

"Talk to me," he whispered, leaning over and putting his lips where his hand rested.

"I can't."

He pulled her shirt out of his way, so his lips could trail farther up her body. He cupped her breast through her bra, and his fingers rolled her nipple.

"Blythe, look at me."

She closed her eyes tighter.

He pulled her shirt back down over her stomach and rolled off the bed. "Come on, then," he said. "Let's get you home."

She opened her eyes. "Why now?"

"You wanted to go. Let's go."

Blythe grabbed her bag and followed him out of the room and to the parking lot. They drove to her house in silence.

Tucker pulled into the driveway, put the truck in park, and unlocked the doors.

"That's it? You're going to drop me off and leave?"

"What do you want, Blythe? You wanted me to bring you home, you're home."

"You don't want to come in?"

"No, I don't."

"Tucker—"

"You're home. Get out of the truck, Blythe."

He hated the look on her face. Hated it. But he hated the feelings warring inside him more. He told her he wanted to talk. He'd been ready then. Now he wasn't. He couldn't pretend the last hour hadn't happened.

"Tucker, please."

"Blythe, if you don't get out of the truck, you're gonna end up going with me, and right now, I don't know where I'm headed."

"Back to Spain?"

He looked away from her.

"Don't leave this way."

Was she kidding? He'd given her every opportunity back at the inn to talk to him. Every opportunity. It was too late in the game for this play. She needed to let him leave.

"I'm going to give you sixty seconds to get out, and if you don't, you're going with me."

"Tucker—"

"Get out of the truck, Blythe. Now."

She did. Thank God. He wasn't sure what he would've done if she hadn't. The door was barely closed before he threw the truck in reverse and peeled out of the driveway.

He saw her in the rearview mirror. The look on her face would haunt him, but he couldn't let himself turn around. He'd been in this situation before, but last time, the girl had gone with him. He'd learned his lesson. It was better to drive away.

As soon as he got far enough from the house that he knew she wouldn't be able to see him, he pulled over. He got out and stopped himself a second before he slammed his fist into the side of the vehicle. That would be all he needed. Work was his only outlet. If he hurt his hand, he'd have nothing.

He'd wanted to talk to her about this thing between them. He wanted to tell her how long it had been since he felt this way about anyone. That he never thought he would again. She had no idea how hard it was for him to come that close to opening up to her.

Why had she gotten upset when he said it was time for him to go home? It was. There were things he needed to take care of. Had she listened, he would've told her that he'd be back, and when he was, he wanted to spend time with her. He'd even started to think about how they could be together all the time. He wasn't sure if that meant she should come to Aspen, or if he would come to Monument.

When she'd asked him about Thanksgiving, he almost felt as though he could tell her the story. If they'd talked about everything else, he may have. Now, he didn't know if he ever would.

He wanted to leave. That was his *modus operandi* after all. Pack. Leave. Repack. Leave again. Get as far away as he could. He'd never found a far away far enough, though.

"Hi," said Bree.

Blythe jumped. She hadn't seen her sister sitting on the front porch.

"Hi."

"He left in an awful big hurry."

"Yeah. I guess I made him mad."

"You guess?"

Blythe couldn't tell if Bree was making a joke by stating the obvious, or asking her a question. She sat down, leaned over, and put her head on her sister's shoulder. Bree hugged her closer.

"I should be comforting you," said Blythe.

"You did plenty of that. My turn to take care of my little sister."

Tears ran down Blythe's cheeks, which only made her feel worse. She was crying because she and Tucker had a fight. He hadn't died, like Zack had. She wiped the tears away with the back of her hand. "I'm sorry, Bree."

"It's okay to cry. There isn't a scorecard. I don't have any more crying points than you do. What happened?"

"I don't know. I just wish he hadn't left."

"Tell him that, right now. Call him, text him, however you can reach him. Tell him. Don't let him leave this way."

"Okay," Blythe whispered. She pulled out her phone and sent Tucker a text, wondering if something like this had happened between Bree and Zack.

I'm sorry, she wrote. *I wish you hadn't left.* She thought for a minute and added, *please give me another chance.*

His phone pinged. Whoever it was, whatever they wanted, he didn't care. He had nothing to give to anyone else right now. As hard as he tried not to look, he couldn't help himself.

Blythe.

Where are you?

What could he say? Around the corner?

Are you at the inn? I'll come over. I have to see you, Tucker. Please don't leave me again.

He stared at the phone. It was one of those moments. He could be stubborn and ignore her. But would that get him anywhere? Would it get him what he wanted? Did he even know what he wanted?

He realized he wasn't standing still any longer. He was walking toward her house. If he cut through the woods, he'd be there in less than two minutes.

Meet me outside, he texted back.

"What?" asked Bree.

"He's coming back."

Bree got up to go inside.

"Wait, you don't have to go."

"Do this, Blythe. Talk to him."

Blythe walked to the end of the driveway and watched for his truck to come back down the road. She was so focused on watching for him, she didn't hear him walk up behind her.

"Blythe," he breathed into her hair.

She spun around and he caught her. "Tucker," she cried. "I'm so sorry."

"I'm sorry, Blythe. I don't know what—"

She didn't let him finish. She reached up and brushed her lips across his. She opened her mouth to him, and he took it. They stood at the end of her driveway, bodies intertwined, mouths locked together, as though they were a couple of teenagers with nowhere else to go.

"Where's your truck?"

"I didn't get very far. I was too pissed to drive, so I pulled over."

"I'm sorry," she said again.

He kissed her forehead. "Blythe, this isn't easy for me. I want us to talk. There are things I want to tell you."

"Okay."

"Okay, what?"

"Let's talk. Do you want to go back to the inn, or do you want to go somewhere else?"

Tucker looked out over the valley in front of them. On the other side of the highway, he could see what looked like a fire road going up the side of Mount Herman.

"Ever been on that road?" he asked.

"Many times. My dad and I go up there and shoot."

"When's the last time you were up there? Is the road open?"

"I don't know, maybe three weeks ago. We haven't had much snow since, so I'm sure it's open."

"Do you need to let anyone know you're leaving again?"

"Nobody saw me, except Bree. She won't say anything."

"Why not?"

"Because she was the one who insisted I tell you I wished you hadn't left."

Tucker nodded his head and took Blythe's hand in his. "Let's go." He led her back through the woods to where he'd left his truck.

What would he say? He wanted to talk, but where should he start? He wanted more in his life; he wanted Blythe to wipe away the bad and replace it with good. He'd spent so many years believing he was incapable of loving or being loved by a woman that, now, he didn't know how to ask for it. It was his damage, as Jace called it.

His brother felt it, that's how Jace knew how to name it. Tucker was damaged. He hadn't allowed himself to consider it would be possible to repair his heart, or his soul. But since he'd met Blythe, he'd felt hope. Even in the light of a tragedy that hit too close, he'd felt hope.

She was quiet, looking out the window as he made his way toward the remote mountain road. She'd practically begged him to come back to the house, to give her another chance. Now that he had, she was waiting for him to talk, to tell her what was so important that her unwillingness to hear him had set him off, made him angry, made him leave.

He was scared; that was the truth of it. What would happen when he talked about the one thing he vowed he never would? Allowing himself to share his past would mean the wound would be ripped open. Would he be able to get through it without breaking down? He doubted it. And when he did, how would Blythe react? Particularly now. She hadn't had any time to process through the grief of the last week. Would she take on his pain too, the way she had her sister's?

No matter what, he couldn't start talking until he found a place to pull off the road.

"You turn here," she said so softly he almost missed it. The paved portion of the road ended, replaced by rough, washboard-ridden dirt. Snow was piled on either side, but the road itself was clear.

When he rounded the bend, the last thing he expected was another car coming from the opposite direction and driving down the center of the narrow road, just like he was.

When he tried to swerve to miss it, his truck hit a patch of ice and careened off into the woods. He frantically tried to turn into it, to keep from skidding further, but he couldn't stop. His truck hit a rock, and he knew they were going to roll. He looked at Blythe. Her terror-filled eyes bored into his. He knew that look. He'd seen it before. The nightmare was repeating itself.

11

Tucker opened his eyes and looked around. He tried to move, but his body wasn't responding to the demands his brain was making. The truck was on an angle, the passenger side, closest to the ground. Blythe's back was to him. She was face down, as though she was looking out the window. He couldn't tell whether or not she was breathing.

The last thing he remembered was the sob of anguish he released, right before the darkness engulfed him again.

When he woke again, he was in a hospital bed. The sights and sounds were hauntingly familiar. He raised his head. Pain. Horrible pain. He felt as though his head was in a vice. He closed his eyes against it.

Blythe. Oh God, what had happened to Blythe? He forced his eyes back open and saw Jace, asleep in the chair next to the bed. He tried to speak, but his mouth was dry and his throat closed up. He could only get out a hoarse sound.

He cleared his throat and tried again. "Jace." This time it was loud enough that his brother woke and stood, coming closer to the bed.

"Hey, man," he said, his own voice clouded with sleep. "How're you doin'?"

"Blythe?"

The flash of a wince on his brother's face told him more than he wanted to know. He had to know the rest. "How bad is it?"

"She's in surgery."

"Answer me. How bad?"

"It's bad, Tuck."

There came the darkness again. This time he welcomed it.

Jace drove up the mountain road, behind the tow truck. He wasn't sure what he'd find, but at the very least, he had to get his brother's personal stuff out his vehicle. He'd made arrangements with the insurance company to have the damage assessed. *Damage.* There was that word again.

When the tow truck stopped, Jace looked up the side of the hill. There it was, on its side. The top of the cab was crushed in. Looking at it, he couldn't believe his brother or Blythe were still alive. Fate had been kinder this time. Much kinder.

Jace sat down on a rock wanting to stay out of the way of the guys trying to figure out how they'd get the truck off the side of the mountain and back down the hill.

The view from this spot was beautiful. Beyond the trees that blanketed the Black Forest, the prairie opened up and spread out all the way to Kansas. To the south, the city of Colorado Springs lay sleepily beyond the confines of the Air Force Academy, and to the north, the skyline of the city of Denver was barely visible. The sky was so blue and the earth, so green around him. If only the beauty of this place had the power to overcome the horrific memories that haunted him.

Tucker blamed himself, carried the guilt around with him day after day. Jace buried it, denied it, tried to force it out of his mind whenever it crept back in. His biggest fear was that, one day, Tucker would feel it and realize it wasn't his own guilt he was feeling; it was Jace's.

"What are you doing?" Jace asked Tucker two days later.

"I'm leaving."

"I know they said you were being released today, but has the doctor been in yet?"

Jace had brought Tucker clothes the night before, anticipating he'd go home today. He came in early enough that he'd be able to see the doctor too and find out what Tuck's aftercare instructions were. His injuries were minimal, which was surprising given the state the truck was in. He'd suffered a concussion, and that was the biggest of Jace's concerns.

"Tuck, what did the doctor say?"

Tucker didn't answer.

"I'm not taking you home until we talk to him. Don't be an asshole. Mama and Daddy are on their way, too."

Tucker sat on the side of the bed. He only had to last a few more hours, maybe as long as a day or two, then he could escape.

He didn't know where he'd go yet. Maybe Mexico. That was his only plan for now. And when he got there, he'd leave Tucker Rice behind. He had no intention of taking his past with him, and that included his name.

Yesterday, his parents told him Blythe was going to be okay. Her appendix ruptured in the accident, and that was why she'd been in surgery. She broke her right arm and right leg, both in several places. She would undergo surgeries to fix them when she was strong enough.

She was alive, but he still had to leave. He didn't have a choice. He got the message. For a brief moment, he had believed he could love again. And then, minutes after he'd allowed himself to hope, it was stripped away. Blythe lived, but he'd heard the warning loud and clear.

The bones in Blythe's right arm and right leg were shattered—multiple breaks and fractures in both. Her face was covered in cuts and abrasions from the truck window that had shattered the same way her bones had.

She woke once and saw someone sitting by her bed. At first she thought it was Tucker, but closed her eyes again when she realized it was Jace.

Her father told her Tucker was okay. He'd suffered a concussion and was expected to be released in a day or two. At least she thought that's what he said. Everything was fuzzy. She couldn't remember whether he'd actually said it or she dreamed it.

When she woke again, Jace was gone and Bree was in the chair he'd been in.

"Hey," Bree said when she noticed Blythe's eyes were open. "How are you feeling, Sleeping Beauty?"

How did she feel? As though she'd been rolled over by a truck. But from what they told her, she'd been inside the truck when it rolled. Sleep was the only relief she could get from the pain.

"Where's Tucker?" she asked, without answering her sister's question.

"He was released today, sweetie."

Released. Maybe he'd come to see her later, or tomorrow. She let herself drift back into sleep. She'd see if someone could call him and ask, after she slept a little bit longer.

Brooke and her husband came to the hospital a little while later, to say goodbye before they went back to Germany. When Brooke lectured her about how none of this would have happened if she hadn't been with Tucker in the first place, Blythe's response was simple. "Get out," she'd said, turned her head, and closed her eyes.

The only thing she wanted to know—and no one seemed to be able to tell her—was where Tucker was.

"How's she doing?"

Blythe pretended to be asleep when she heard Jace talking to Bree.

"She's getting there. She's stopped asking about him."

"We don't know where he is," Jace whispered.

"What do you mean?"

"He left the day after he got out of the hospital. It isn't unlike him, but…"

"Finish your sentence," Bree insisted.

"He usually checks in by now, and he hasn't. My parents are worried sick. So am I, to be honest."

"Why would he leave? Doesn't he care how Blythe is? For Christ's sake, it's his fault she's here."

Blythe winced. It had been an accident. It wasn't Tucker's fault. She almost said so, but stayed quiet. She wanted to hear what Jace had to say if he continued.

"That's why he's gone. It's the second time this has happened."

"Come with me," she heard Bree say. Blythe wanted to stop them so she could hear the rest, but something told her it was a story she didn't want to hear. Instead, she turned her head and went back to sleep.

Blythe was going home, but she'd be back in a week for surgery on her arm. Not long after, they'd operate on her leg. It had been explained to her more than once, but she was too groggy from the pain meds to understand much of what they were telling her.

Instead of going to the house in Palmer Lake, the one she'd planned to share with Lyric, she went to her parents' house. She felt bad, but with everything she still had in front of her, she'd need their help.

Every morning, her parents pushed her to do physical therapy, which she hated. When Bree was with her, she'd let her slack off. Bree would spend the hour talking instead of making her do her exercises.

"You have to have surgery again anyway," she'd say. "You can do the physical therapy after."

Renie visited, but she didn't bring Willow with her. She was afraid the little girl would be too rambunctious.

"You could stay longer if you brought her. As it is, you have to leave an hour after you get here."

"I'll bring her next time," Renie would say, but she never did.

Lyric, who had settled into the house in Palmer Lake by herself, came to see Blythe almost every day. She was able to do some RodeoChat work, until either the pain got so bad that she couldn't concentrate anymore, or she'd take something for it that made her groggy.

Jace came to see her almost every day, too. She never asked him about Tucker. She had no idea what he'd wanted to talk to her about before the accident, but it didn't matter now. As he had before, he left. She didn't blame him for the accident, but it hurt that he didn't care whether she was okay or not.

"How about a movie today, maybe get some lunch afterwards?" Jace tried to get her to go out, get some fresh air, but she didn't feel up to it. Until her leg healed more, she had to use a wheelchair to get around. The cast on her arm went all the way from her shoulder to her wrist. It was uncomfortable, and it made her miserable.

It didn't seem to matter to Jace. He took her bad moods in stride, which only made her more irritated with him.

"Listen, you don't have to come see me. I'm fine. Aren't you supposed to be out, chasing girls on the rodeo circuit or something?"

When he laughed, Blythe wanted to punch him.

"Billy and I will be headin' out soon enough, and we'll be chasin' eight seconds more than girls, darlin'."

"Billy maybe, but you can't convince me you aren't gonna be hooking up with a buckle bunny or two."

"You been talkin' to Lyric or somethin'?"

As a matter of fact, she had. And it was Lyric who'd asked her why Jace was hanging around so much.

"You two together again?"

Again? No, they weren't together again, because they'd never been together in the first place. How could Lyric even ask her that? She'd had sex with Tucker, for God's sake. And honestly, being around Jace was becoming harder and harder. It hurt to look at him because, obviously, he reminded her of Tucker. They were twins.

Whenever she thought about him, she got angry, and then she'd take it out on Jace. The meaner she got, the nicer he was. When he left, he'd kiss her forehead, or her cheek, and it drove her crazy.

"I don't want you to visit me anymore," she would tell him at least every few days.

It never stopped him. He might take a day or two off, but then he'd be back, as though nothing had been said between them.

Blythe asked her mother to put a call in to her doctor. The medicine she was taking was making her nauseous, and she wanted to see if he could switch her to something else. Instead of calling in a different prescription, he asked Paige to bring her into the office.

"Why does he have to make it so complicated? Has he ever been in a damn wheelchair? Does he have any idea how hard it is for me to come into his office? Why couldn't he just call something in?"

"I don't know, baby." No matter how nice anyone was to her, it irritated Blythe, and that included her mother.

When the doctor asked her to pee in a cup, Blythe was ready to take his head off.

"Is he kidding?" she asked after he left the examination room. "How in the hell am I supposed to do that?" She pointed to her right arm, the one in the cast, and then at her leg. "Somehow I'm supposed to be able to hold a cup and pee in it?"

"I think you'll need help, sweetheart," Paige answered.

"I spent the first two weeks needing to have someone help me every time I had to use the bathroom. I'm tired of it. Forget it. Let's go. I'll take Tylenol."

Paige wouldn't budge and made Blythe give the doctor a urine sample. "You'll get through this."

Blythe wished she'd asked Bree to come with her rather than her mother. Bree was easier on her. She might've even been able to talk Bree into giving the sample for her, so she didn't have to.

They'd been waiting for over a half hour when the doctor finally came back in. Blythe started to say something, but stopped when her mother put her hand on Blythe's good shoulder and squeezed.

He sat down on the stool and wheeled it closer to her.

"Blythe, there's something we need to talk about, and it's fairly serious. Would you like your mom to step out?"

"No, it's okay. She can stay."

As if everything she was going through wasn't serious enough. What now? Her leg wasn't healing properly? She had to have another surgery? What did that have to do with peeing in a cup?

Paige sat down. Why was her mother sitting down? And why did she look so pale? Blythe turned back to the doctor.

"Well, what is it? Spit it out, for Christ's sake."

"You're pregnant."

Oh my God. That wasn't what she'd expected him to say. Was he joking? Did he say that because she was being such a bitch? She looked into his eyes. It didn't look like he was bullshitting her.

"That's impossible."

"Are you saying you haven't had sexual relations in the last few months?"

What was he saying? Her mother was in the room. "Yes, I have," she answered as quietly as she could. "But I'm on the pill."

"Are you still taking it?"

Well, no. She hadn't been, not since the accident. But she also hadn't had sex since the accident.

"Do you remember when you stopped taking it?"

She thought back. It was a blur. Between being with Bree when Zack died, and the funeral...all the traveling. *Oh no.* She couldn't remember taking the pills with her to California. And then, with everything going on, she hadn't remembered to take one since.

"As I suspected," he said without her needing to answer. "I would guess you're close to two months along."

"More like three," she answered. It didn't take a genius to figure it out. She'd only been with Tucker one day…and night…and then the next day. Then they'd gotten into the accident. The math was easy.

"It makes what we have to talk about even more urgent."

"What?"

"Blythe," he began. "You need to consider the trauma your body has been through in the last three months. You've had multiple surgeries, medications, x-rays…"

"What are you saying?"

"The fetus may have been compromised. We didn't take any of the precautions we would've, had we known you were pregnant."

Compromised? What the hell did that mean?

"There are tests we can run, certainly, but this early in the pregnancy, we can't be sure any will be indicative of how the baby will be as we get closer to full term."

Blythe stopped listening. She was pregnant with Tucker's baby.

"I'm sure you'll want to give it some thought. Give the office a call to schedule an appointment when you've decided what you'd like to do. You can also call this number if you have any questions." The doctor wrote a phone number on the back of a business card and handed it to her. "That's my private service. If you leave a message with them, I'll call you back as soon as I'm able to."

"I've already made my decision."

"Blythe—"

"It's okay, Mom. It doesn't matter what any test says, I'm having this baby." It was Tucker's baby, and she was having it. She rubbed her good hand over her belly.

"There are things you should consider," the doctor continued.

"There isn't anything for me to *consider*. I've made up my mind, and my decision is final."

"I have to warn you, there is still a chance the baby will abort itself and you'll have a miscarriage. As I said, we have no way of knowing what kind of damage the fetus has sustained."

Damage. That's what Jace had said about Tucker, that he was damaged. Blythe knew there was nothing wrong with their baby. The baby wasn't damaged. No one could tell her otherwise.

Blythe sent a text to Jace on the way home, asking him to meet her at the house. His truck was in the driveway when they pulled in.

"Hey, you," he said, walking up to her mother's car. He reached in and picked her up.

"You don't have to carry me."

"I don't? Gotta tell ya, it's easier to carry you than it is to push that damn wheelchair."

He had a point.

"Where were you?"

"At the doctor."

He kicked the front door open with his foot and carried her over to the couch in the living room.

"How did it go? Any news on the next surgery?"

"No, but there's other news."

"What's that?"

No point in beating around the bush. Maybe this news would push Jace and his parents to try harder to find Tucker.

"I'm pregnant."

Jace felt the air leave his lungs. He wasn't sure how long it took before he was able to take another breath. Blythe was pregnant. *Jesus.*

"Nothing to say?" she asked.

"Taking it in."

"Where is Tucker?"

"I have no idea, Blythe. I wish I did."

"You better figure it out."

He heard her. She wanted him to find Tucker. He understood. He hoped and prayed he'd be able to. He had no idea where to even start.

* * *

Todos Santos. Not deep enough into Mexico, but it was a starting point. Tucker got a job as a bartender, not that he needed a job from a cash standpoint, but he needed enough of a cover to blend in, so no one paid attention to him. There were studio apartments available for resort staff, so he had a place to live.

He longed to paint, but he never stayed sober long enough to do it. He drank as much liquor as he poured for guests of the resort, yet it was never enough. When he felt the air leave his lungs, he poured another drink, sinking further into his drunken stupor. It didn't matter what Jace was feeling, only that he prevented himself from feeling it too.

* * *

Jace was outside in the driveway, making a phone call when Bree pulled up. He thought about pretending he was actually having a conversation with someone, but why?

"Hi," he said, giving her a head nod.

"Hi," she answered, looking as annoyed by him as she always did.

"I guess Blythe is back, since you're here."

Maybe he should've pretended he was talking to someone since she seemed even bitchier today than usual.

"Who are you calling?"

"My parents…" He'd actually thought about telling her it wasn't any of her business, another thing he normally wouldn't have said to anybody.

"I can't believe that you expect Blythe to believe you still don't know where he is. Stop lying to her, Jace. Tell her the truth so she can move on with her life, without either you or your brother in it."

"I would expect that to be the last thing you'd want for her. Don't you think she should have someone in her life to help her raise the baby—" Jace knew in an instant that Bree hadn't known Blythe was pregnant, and he'd just put his big foot in it.

"What are you talking about?"

What could he say now? He'd already as much as told her. "Blythe is pregnant."

Bree stormed around him, went in the front door of the house, and slammed it behind her.

"You're sure you're pregnant, and you're sure you want to have this baby?" she asked Blythe after her sister told her about her appointment with the doctor.

"Absolutely sure, Bree. I don't care what anyone says. I know there isn't anything wrong. I can feel it."

"You can feel the baby?"

"Yes...no. I mean, I can't feel it moving or anything. I just know. I know you don't believe me, but...it doesn't matter whether anyone believes me or not. I'm not changing my mind."

"I'm not saying you should. I asked if you were sure. I'm not trying to talk you in or out of anything, Blythe."

"Good."

"By the way, I stopped to see Lyric on my way here."

"Yeah?"

"She asked me if I wanted to move in with her, at least temporarily."

"That's a great idea! I feel terrible that I left her roommate-less, and while I'm going to miss seeing you every day, I do think it's for the best. You're here, but you're not *here*, if you know what I mean."

Bree smiled and leaned in to hug Blythe.

"I'm jealous though. I love that sweet house in the Palmer Lake Glen."

The house was built on the side of a hill, and behind it was a trail that went up Sundance Mountain to the reservoirs above the town, and had been the first place their family lived in when they moved to Colorado.

The small town had once been a vacation spot for the Vail family, who did their best to gentrify it. In the 1920s, they established the Rocky Mountain

Chautauqua Assembly, making Palmer Lake a destination point for many travelers.

It had suffered from the drought in the last couple of years, and the town struggled to maintain its former glory, without much success. However, the beauty remained, making it one of the nicest places to live on the Rampart Range. The holiday traditions were a big part of what made Palmer Lake so special—and, despite the difficult economic climate, they remained.

During the Great Depression, the town's residents had erected a five-hundred-foot, five-point star on the side of Sundance Mountain, above the lake. Each year since then, the star was lit the entire month of December.

"Remember looking for the yule log?" Blythe asked.

"Every year."

"Could Dad see them hiding it from the back windows?"

"I don't know. What makes you think he could?"

"I can't imagine it was a coincidence that he found it three years in a row."

When Blythe and her sisters were little, they'd join as many as five hundred people on the annual hunt for the Yule Log—another Palmer Lake tradition, started by the Vail family in the 1930s. The hunt was held the first weekend of December and started at the town hall, where residents would gather, sing Christmas carols, and drink wassail and hot chocolate before donning red and green capes to begin their trek into the forest.

Sometimes it took a few minutes to find the eight-foot notched log, and sometimes it took as long as an hour or two. Whoever found it was given the honor of riding it, pulled by ropes held by other revelers, back up the steep road to the town hall. Three times in her life, her father had been the one to find it, so she and her sisters got to ride the log.

"I never thought about it, but maybe you're right. I'd hate to think Dad would cheat, but he probably did it so each of us could have their turn riding up the hill."

"That's what I was thinking. Anyway, you've decided to move in with Lyric. I think it's a great idea. When?"

"Tonight."

"That soon?" Blythe shouldn't be surprised. Bree couldn't stay with her parents forever; she was a grown woman. She wasn't like Blythe, who still hadn't moved out on her own.

12

"The baby isn't your responsibility, Jace." Blythe wished Bree was here this morning instead of at the house in the glen. Whenever he started in on her about something, Bree would jump in and tell him to leave her alone.

"What if I want to make it my responsibility? I care about you, and I care about the baby. Let me do this, Blythe. Let me be part of your lives."

"Jace, you have to understand—"

"I know what you're gonna say, and it's okay."

"What was I going to say?"

"That you're not over Tucker. It's okay. I can wait."

"It isn't that I'm not over him. I'm having his baby, Jace. Doesn't that kind of...I don't know...turn you off of me?"

Jace touched the side of her face. "No, it doesn't. I meant what I said. I want to be part of your lives. And if you don't feel the same way about me as I feel about you, well, I'll learn to be patient."

"What if I never feel the way you do, Jace?"

"You did once, Blythe. I know you did. Things got all kinds of mixed up between you and me and Tuck.

But I'm here now, and he isn't. I asked you once before, and I'll ask you again. Please, give me a chance. That's all I'm askin' for. A chance."

"And if I say no?"

"I'll ignore ya."

"That's what I figured," she laughed. "But Jace, I have to be honest with you. I think I knew from the first day I met you and Tucker that he was the man for me. I'm sorry if I gave you a different impression."

"I know that, Blythe." He leaned forward and kissed her forehead. "But I'm not givin' up."

"What does that mean?"

"For now, I'll be your friend—your best friend. I'll be here when you need me. I'll help you with the pregnancy, and once the baby's here, I'll help you then, too. I'm here for you, Blythe. That's all you need to know right now."

"You're sure about this?"

"Never more sure of anything."

The ultrasounds they performed indicated Blythe's baby seemed perfectly healthy. She was far enough along that they should have been able to tell the baby's sex, but Blythe insisted she didn't want to know.

The doctors wanted to perform an amniocentesis soon, saying it would give them information the ultrasound could not. Blythe hadn't decided whether to do the test or not. There were risks that the doctors said were minimal, but any risk was too much. Blythe didn't want to put their baby through anything else—how he or she had survived this long was a miracle.

More often, Blythe found herself turning to Jace when she had to make a decision about the baby. She listened to her parents when they gave their opinion, and to Bree, and even Renie. But when the time came to make a decision, it was Jace whom Blythe listened to.

He was the one who convinced her to consider the amniocentesis. Whatever they learned, he told her, they'd face together. Ultimately, if there were anything wrong—and he was sure there wasn't—it would give them a chance to do more to help the baby.

Three weeks later, Blythe received the results. These tests, too, were very positive. She started calling the baby "Miracle," and so did Jace.

He was always close, affectionate, but not in a romantic way. When Blythe was with him, she was calm. When he wasn't around, she grew anxious. Everyone sensed it, especially Jace.

Sunday afternoon Paige and Mark were hosting a barbecue, and the Cochran house was full. Billy and Renie were staying at the ranch in Black Forest, so they came over. Ben and Liv flew in for a visit and brought Jace's parents with them. They wanted to see Blythe and let her know they would support her in any way they could.

Jace could feel Blythe's exhaustion from all the activity in the other room. She needed him. He could feel it. Billy was in the middle of a sentence Jace wasn't listening to anyway, when he walked away.

He sat down next to her and drew her into him. As much as he knew he shouldn't, he was falling in love with Blythe. He didn't know if she'd ever love him the way he loved her, but it didn't matter; he'd never leave her. His brother had, but he wouldn't.

Blythe rested her head on his shoulder.

"You're exhausted, sweetheart."

For now, Blythe was staying in the guest room on the main floor of the house. Next week, she was scheduled to have the cast removed from her arm, and if all went as planned, she'd be able to stop using the wheelchair shortly after.

"Time for you to get some rest," Jace said, picking her up and carrying her into the bedroom.

"Maybe she wasn't tired." Bree met him when he came back out the bedroom door.

"Blythe was beyond tired, Bree."

"She has a mind of her own, you know."

"She does that."

"You know she doesn't want you here."

It was one thing for Blythe to say it, because he knew that half the time she tried to push him away, she did it because she believed it was for his own good. Hearing it from her sister hurt, far worse than he would've expected it to. Jace tried to walk away, but Bree grabbed his arm.

"I don't like the way you treat her."

"I couldn't care less what you like or don't like," Jace growled at her. "The only thing I care about is the woman on the other side of this door. The one who needs rest. Now get the hell out of my way before our arguing wakes her up."

Jace stormed past her, unintentionally bumping her into the wall when he did. Bree wasn't with Blythe every waking hour like he was. He'd had just about enough of her telling him anything about the woman he'd promised to take care of for the rest of her life.

Before Bree could follow, her mother stepped in her way. "Let it go."

"He doesn't let her think for herself," Jace heard Bree say to Paige.

"He's exactly what she needs right now. Let it go. I won't say it again."

Jace watched Bree go out the front door. Maybe she was leaving—that wouldn't bother him one bit. He went in the opposite direction, out the slider to the deck.

"What the hell?" he said, seeing Bree sitting in one of the Adirondack chairs. "Are you followin' me?"

"I was out here *first*, cowboy. So it's you following me."

"You're 'bout the last person on earth I would want to follow, so you can let go of that fantasy. I thought you went out the front door."

Her face turned red, and she clenched and unclenched her fists, as though she wanted to hit him.

"You're such an…*asshole*," she spat.

Jace opened the slider to go back inside. "Been called worse, darlin'."

Bree opened and closed her mouth a few times, he guessed trying to come up with something that might actually offend him. He was beyond being offended by anything this lady had to say to him. She'd hurt him a few minutes ago, but he wouldn't let her do it again. He had too many other things to worry about.

He had to find Tucker, and so far, he had nothing to go on. Tuck hadn't been seen along any of his usual escape routes, there was no activity on his bank account, and he wasn't using his credit cards. No matter what he decided to do once he knew, Tucker was entitled to know he was going to be a father. Half of him hoped he'd come back and be the man Blythe needed him to be. The other half hoped he'd stay gone. And what kind of man did that make him?

Blythe couldn't sleep, mainly because the baby couldn't either. He, she liked to think he was a boy, couldn't find a comfortable place to rest, so he was doing somersaults in her stomach. She reached over and turned on the light, bringing her sweatshirt up, and leaving her belly bare.

Every so often, a part of him would press against her, and she could see the slight movement on the surface of her stomach. When she rested her hand there, he'd stop moving, as though he could feel his mother's hand comforting him.

"Why aren't you asleep?" Jace asked.

He startled her; she'd been concentrating on watching the baby, and hadn't heard him come in. "Miracle baby woke me up."

He walked over and rested his hand on top of hers, as he so often did. He leaned down and kissed her belly.

"Go to sleep, miracle baby. Let your mama get some rest."

Why couldn't she love him? There were days she was certain Tucker would never come back, but Jace? He was right here, in front of her. Gentle, loving, nurturing, and patient. He said he'd never run out of patience, but what if she never felt the way he did?

He reached up and rubbed his fingers over her forehead. "So much worry tonight. What's goin' on?"

"I'm worried about you."

"We've talked about this. Nothin' to worry about where I'm concerned, darlin'. Nothin' at all. You're my life now. You and this little baby."

"What if I can't be what you want me to be?"

"Blythe, how many times do we have to talk about this?"

She didn't need to answer him. He knew what she was saying, and she was right. Every night, when he finally let the sleep he fought take over, he dreamed of her. It was often the same dream. He was making love to her, and each time, she called out Tucker's name. It would wake him up, and he'd fight going back to sleep again.

***

Even through his drunken haze, Tucker felt his brother's warring emotions. He'd alternate between serenity and anguish. When Tucker felt Jace's peace, he wondered if that meant he and Blythe were together. But what about the anguish? What was that about? Or was it his own anguish he felt? The lines were so blurred he couldn't tell where he ended and Jace began.

13

Blythe asked Bree to take her out to Billy's ranch to watch him and Jace train. Billy and Renie would be leaving for Crested Butte soon, where Renie and Willow would stay with Liv and Ben while Billy was on the road. Jace would follow shortly after. Blythe wanted to spend as much time with all of them as she could before they left.

Jace told her he was thinking about quitting saddle bronc riding so he could stay home with her. She told him, if he did that, she would never speak to him again. It was bad enough that he spent most of his time with her; she wouldn't let him give up something he'd worked so hard for.

He made her promise to come and watch him practice, and to come to some of the rodeos he was competing in. She agreed, particularly when Lyric said it would be a great opportunity for RodeoChat, and she'd go with her.

They were already planning when they'd join everyone in Crested Butte for the big rodeo in Gunnison's Cattlemen's Days.

"Hey, Jace, don't you have a place in Aspen?" Blythe asked.

"I do, darlin'. You plannin' a little getaway?"

"No, but Bree is going to the X Games. I thought, if it was empty, she could stay there. She's having a hard time finding a place with rooms available."

"I'll find a place, Blythe. I can always stay in Basalt and drive in every day."

"Why're you goin' to the X Games?"

"Tell him, Bree. I think what you're doing is really cool."

"I'm researching why people participate in extreme sports."

"There's more. Go ahead, tell him," Blythe prodded.

"I'm thinking of interviewing people who ride bulls and broncs, even barrel racers."

"Jace, why don't you let Bree interview you?"

Why didn't Bree ask herself, if she wanted to interview him? He knew the answer—because she didn't. Blythe was trying hard to make peace between them, like she was doing now, and he hated to disappoint her, but he and Bree barely tolerated one another. She took every opportunity to tell him he didn't have a place in Blythe's life.

"Blythe's *family* is perfectly capable of taking care of her," she'd say. "You don't need to be here every day.

Let her get back to a normal life." Bree worked that into almost every conversation she had with him.

"Can you explain how me leavin' her alone makes her life normal? She's pregnant, twenty-three years old, the father of her baby is God knows where and doesn't even know he's going to be a father, but it's me that makes her life abnormal." Jace had shaken his head and walked away after that conversation. Actually, he shook his head and walked away after every conversation he had with Blythe's sister.

"Yeah, well, if you can't find a place, you can stay in the condo in Aspen. Lemme know. Billy's waitin' to get started." That was a crock of shit; Billy never waited on anyone.

"Never seen a woman rattle you that way," Billy goaded him.

"She doesn't rattle me. She makes my skin crawl."

"Whatever," Billy smirked.

"You ready to get back to work? If not, I'll let you gossip with the girls sittin' over there." Jace motioned toward the barn, where Renie, Blythe, and Bree sat, watching them.

Billy laughed, which made Jace want to knock him into the dirt, but that would happen soon enough without Jace having to do it. This weekend they'd be in Pueblo, and the horse Billy was due to ride had bucked off its last fifteen riders. Jace was as thankful he hadn't drawn that horse, as he would be to see Billy eat a little dirt.

The baby was kicking up a storm. Sometimes it hurt, but most times it tickled. Like it was now. Blythe started to giggle. Renie and Bree were used to it. If she was laughing and rubbing her belly, they knew why.

"Can I feel?" Bree asked her.

"Of course, you don't have to ask. I don't like strangers touching my belly—which happens more than you'd think—but you can, whenever you want."

Blythe watched her sister's face turn from troubled to serene when she felt the baby kick. Was she wishing she and Zack had gotten pregnant before he was deployed? At least then she wouldn't be alone.

Lyric drove up and parked next to where they were sitting. Things would get interesting now. They always did when Lyric was around. She never hesitated to say exactly what was on her mind, which usually resulted in the four of them laughing hysterically.

They formed their own tight-knit circle. Renie wasn't around as often, between finishing school and raising Willow, who was growing like a weed. She was eighteen months old, walking and talking like a little lady.

"Come here and see Auntie Blythe, Willow. You wanna feel my baby?"

Willow toddled over, and Blythe showed her where to rest her hands. When Willow felt the baby move, she jumped, and then started to giggle. Was there a better sound on earth than a little girl's giggle?

Jace watched Blythe playing with Willow. When she was around the little girl, she never stopped smiling. She told him she was worried about what kind of mother she'd be, but she'd be a great one. All she lacked was confidence. Once her baby was born, she'd be too busy to over-think herself.

Her baby. Not their baby. As close as he felt to her, and as much as he loved that bundle growing inside her, the baby would never be his. He'd always be Uncle Jace.

He caught Bree's eye instead of Blythe's. She was watching him. He watched her too, when she wasn't looking. Why did she irritate him so much? Every time she opened her damned mouth, he wanted to throttle her.

Lyric walked over. "I wanna do a spotlight on you and Billy this week. Different than the interview we did on him at the National Western. This time the focus would be on him retiring, you gettin' started on broncs. RodeoChat followers would love to hear your different perspectives, especially since ya'll are travelin' together. That's weird on its own."

He'd heard that Billy never had a travel partner when he was competing hardcore. Jace figured it was because no one wanted to be around the guy. He'd also heard Billy believed it was bad luck. They hadn't talked about it, but Billy was riding great, so evidently, he'd stopped believing his own superstition.

"Sure, Lyric. You know we're happy to talk to you anytime."

"Bree's gonna sit in on it, too. She's got some questions of her own about some research project she's doin'. If you ask me, that sociology stuff is a load of crap, but what do I know?"

Jace scratched his chin, wishing he'd seen that one coming. Too late to bow out now, though. "She mentioned somethin' about it, but I didn't get the impression she was interested in anything I had to say."

Lyric shook her head and looked over at Bree. "You're so wrong, cowboy. Bree is interested in *everything* you have to say."

The interview hadn't exactly gone the way Jace expected. Instead of Bree asking him about bronc riding, Lyric went in a completely different direction, asking him whether he believed twins had a connection unlike other siblings.

"When was the first time you realized you knew what your brother was thinking?" she asked.

Jace wished Bree wasn't part of this conversation. He didn't mind sharing this stuff with Lyric; she was a twin. She understood in a way Bree never would.

"I don't know, exactly, it was always that way. Not so much that I knew what he was thinking, it was more what he was feeling."

"Do you know what he's feeling now?" Bree asked.

He did, but he wasn't sure he could put it into words. Conflicted, but it was so much more than that.

He shrugged. "Not really."

"Did you and Tucker ever talk about it—knowing how the other was feeling?" she asked.

"All the time," he laughed. "Especially when we met your sister." Why had he said that?

"You both love her, don't you?"

That question took him by surprise. Based on how often Bree tried to kick him out of Blythe's life, he doubted she knew the depth of his feelings for her sister.

"We do, but not in the same way."

"It's exactly the same way," she murmured.

She was probably right, but he'd already said more than he wished he had. Bree had enough ammunition that she never hesitated to use against him. Her acknowledging his love for Blythe made him feel more vulnerable than ever.

"What if he never comes back?"

"I don't know, Bree."

"Do you think he knows how you're feeling? About Blythe, I mean? Do you think he knows you're in love with her?"

"I'm sure he does."

"How do you do it?" she whispered.

"What choice do I have?"

"You could leave, too."

"Never." It was that simple. He'd never leave. He'd promised Blythe he'd be there for her and the baby, and he would be. It didn't matter if she pushed him away, he'd just keep coming back.

"You got another question for me, or are we finished here?"

"One more, Jace. What if he does come back?"

How could he answer that question? He missed his brother so much he ached. He also ached for Blythe. Even if Tuck did come back, his damage would come with him. Tucker would always hold a part of himself back because of what happened on Thanksgiving all those years ago.

"Jace?"

"We're done here." He stood and walked away.

* * *

Tucker dreamed about Blythe almost every time he closed his eyes. The more he drank, the weirder his dreams got. They were becoming illogical, jumbled up things he couldn't understand.

He still dreamed about another woman, but she and Blythe melded together, becoming the same person. After the accident, he understood why.

* * *

"I can't go home," Blythe told Bree a couple of days later.

"Why not?"

"You know how Mom gets. She's driving me crazy."

"I could try to smooth things out if you want."

"No, I want to move in with you and Lyric."

"You do? When?"

"Now, Bree. Aren't you listening?"

"Okay, sorry. Let me rephrase. Would you like to go straight there, or go home and pack?"

"Let's go tell Lyric, and then go home and pack."

"You've got to be kidding," they heard Lyric say when she walked into the house in the glen.

"Jesus, Bullet. What the hell is wrong with you?"

Lyric motioned that she'd just be a minute.

"I can't help you with this one, bro. You're on your own. I warned you the last time I wouldn't intervene again. I gotta go, my roommate's here. I'll talk to ya later, Bullet."

Lyric tossed her phone on the counter and put her head in her hands. "Sorry, that boy just works my last nerve. What's up, girls?"

"I want to move in."

"Oh, yeah? That's awesome. I've been thinking about this. Let's get me moved, and then we can go get your stuff."

"Why are you moving?" Bree asked.

"I'm not movin' out, just movin' rooms."

"Why?" Bree asked again.

"The room I'm in shares a bathroom with the room we aren't using. Blythe should have my room."

"My turn," Blythe laughed. "Why, Lyric?"

"We gotta start thinkin' about settin' up a nursery." Lyric shook her head and pointed at Blythe. "She's pregnant, so she gets a pass. But damn, Bree, for somebody so dang smart, you sure are slow about certain things."

"I just love her, don't you, Bree?" Blythe had learned a while ago, it was best to just go along with whatever Lyric suggested, even if it seemed crazy. In the end, her ideas were always good ones.

"Don't just stand there, come help me." When Blythe got up, Lyric pushed her back in the chair. "Not you."

"What are you doing?" Jace asked when he walked up and saw Bree and Lyric carrying boxes to Lyric's car.

"Movin' Blythe to Palmer Lake," Lyric answered.

"Why?"

"She's ready."

"But she's going to have to move again."

"What are you talking about?" Bree's arms were full of clothes still on their hangers. She looked back and forth between Jace and Lyric, who were both standing empty-handed. "Could one of you open the door for me?"

"Of course, sorry." They both moved in the direction of the car at the same time. Lyric stepped back and let Jace open it.

"Why would Blythe have to move again?" Bree asked.

"Don't worry, I switched rooms. We're ready for her," Lyric answered before Jace could.

"What are you talking about, Lyric?" Jace was ready to pound his head against the side of the house.

"I moved out of the big room, the one that's connected to the smaller one. It's got a bathroom between them."

"She and the baby are going to live with me."

Bree was almost in the house when he said it. She stopped and turned around slowly. "What do you mean, they're going to live with you?"

"How many things can that mean, Bree?"

He'd seen her mad but never as mad as she looked now.

"What is with you? Have you ever, once, considered asking anyone else what he or she wants to do? Or are you in the habit of making decisions no one asked you to make?"

"Blythe and I have discussed this."

"You have? And what did she say about it? Because, the last time I checked, *she* was the one who told us she wanted to move to Palmer Lake."

Jace stormed in the house, looking for Blythe. He found her sitting on the bed, crying.

"What's wrong?" He sank to his knees in front of her.

"Why won't he come home?"

He wished he had an answer, but he didn't. When he put his arms around her, she cried harder.

"What have you done now?" Bree asked from the doorway.

He ignored her.

"Blythe, honey, what's wrong?" Bree sat down on the bed, next to her sister and rubbed her back.

"Tucker," Jace spit out.

"How could he have left without even saying good-bye?" Blythe cried.

"I wish I could tell you—" Jace noticed Bree was crying too. "What's wrong with you?" He cringed. That sounded worse than he'd meant it.

Bree opened her mouth as though she was going to say something, but turned and left the room instead.

"You shouldn't be so mean to her," Blythe whispered.

"I'm not mean to her."

"You are. I've never seen you be mean to anyone, Jace, but you're mean to my sister. She lost her husband a few months ago. It would do you good to remember that. You could be kind, you know."

Blythe wiggled herself free of him. "Go apologize."

The last thing he wanted to do was apologize to Blythe's bitch of a sister, but he supposed he had to.

Blythe shoved him. "Go."

He looked around the house, but didn't see her. Just when he was about to go back and tell Blythe he couldn't find her, he saw her huddled on a bench on the back deck. Her head was down, but he could tell by the way her body shook, she was crying.

He opened the sliding door and crept out. "I'm sorry."

"Go away, Jace."

"Can't do that. I made you cry, and I didn't mean to. So, I'm here to apologize."

"You didn't make me cry. Don't give yourself that much credit."

If it were up to him, he'd go back in the house, but if he did, Blythe would be mad at him.

"Come on, now," he knelt down in front of her, put his hands on her arms, and pulled them away from her body. He kept pulling until her head rested on his shoulder. She didn't wrap her arms around him, but she didn't move away from him either.

"What's going on out there?" Lyric asked Blythe.

"I'm not sure. Something Jace said made Bree cry, so I told him to apologize."

"I've been watching them for full-on five minutes, and she hasn't stopped crying. Jeez, what did he say?"

"I don't know. She started to cry and ran out of the room. Were they arguing before he came inside?"

"Yeah, but only about where you were going to live. She was harder on him than he was on her."

"Shh," he whispered, trying to match his breathing with hers. "What happened in there?"

"Leave me alone." She pulled away and put her hands over her face.

Jace put his hands on her wrists. "Bree, you and I don't get along—that's no secret—but whatever I said, I'm sorry for. I sure didn't mean to make you cry."

"It isn't you." She tried to jerk her hands away, but he wouldn't let go.

"Then, tell me who it is."

"It's none of your business."

"I'm makin' it my business. Isn't that what you always accuse me of, not listening to what anyone else wants? I want you to tell me what's got you cryin' so hard, and I'm not givin' up until you tell me. I'm a stubborn SOB, and I'll stay on my knees in front of you until you tell me. I don't care how long it takes."

He moved her her wrists so he could grip both with one hand. He put his other palm on the side of her face and gently turned her head so she faced him. "Come on, tell me, so I don't do it again."

"It doesn't have anything to do with you. I already told you that. You don't listen."

"Somethin' I said set you off, so let's get this out in the open. I'm giving you free rein here, darlin'. You've never held back on tellin' what you think before. Have at it. I'm wide open. Give it your best shot."

That made her smile. At least he was getting somewhere. "Bree," he looked in her eyes while his finger stroked her cheek. "Tell me."

When tears slid down her face, he let go of her wrists and pulled her into him.

"We had a fight," she said into his shoulder.

"We always fight, darlin'. I didn't think you liked me enough to cry about it."

"Not you. *Zack.*"

Oh, shit. "What happened?"

"He left, like Tucker. We didn't…"

"Go ahead, keep talkin'. Get it out."

"We apologized, over the phone. But…"

Bree was crying again, harder than she had before.

Jace slid one arm under her knees and put the other behind her back. As gently as he could, he lifted her up far enough that he could sit on the bench with her. As he lowered himself, he cradled her on his lap and wrapped his arms around her tighter.

14

Jace didn't know how long they'd been on the deck, but Bree's skin felt like ice. She'd finally stopped crying and was so still against him that he didn't want to move.

"I'm sorry," she whispered.

He closed his eyes. "Don't be."

"You don't like me."

"I like you more than you like me."

"That's probably true."

His cheek rested against her hair. "You're cold; let's get you inside."

"Two more minutes?"

"Tell you what, let's make it five, darlin'." Even though he couldn't see it, he'd be willing to bet she smiled.

"What's going on?" Paige asked Blythe and Lyric who were still standing by the window.

"I don't know, but it looks like he's gotten her to stop crying."

"Let me see." Lyric moved so Paige could look out the window.

"What is he doing? She hates him."

"Hate might be too strong of a word, Mom."

"Okay, she doesn't like him."

"Fine line between love and hate they say," added Lyric.

"Huh," Paige said again. "Wish we could hear what they're talking about."

Five minutes passed, but Jace still didn't want to move.

He heard the door open and felt her body tense. It was Mark, who dropped a blanket on the bench, and then lit the outdoor heater, scooting it closer to them before he went back inside. With one hand, Jace opened the blanket and tucked it around her. She'd gone so still, he wondered if she had fallen asleep.

A few minutes later, she woke up with a start. She tried to get up, but Jace wouldn't let her.

"What are you doing? Let go of me."

"Nope, not gonna do that." He tightened his grip. "We're gonna come to an understanding before I let you go."

"Here we go…"

"Now, see what you do? You always assume the worst about me. I wonder why that is."

"Maybe because you're so bossy."

"I don't think anyone has ever accused me of bein' bossy as much as you. I'm thinkin' you take me wrong."

"You won't let me get up. How should I take that?"

He kissed her hairline, right on the edge of her forehead. "You could take it that I like holdin' on to you."

"I doubt that," she laughed.

"Bree," he breathed.

"Don't."

"Don't what?"

"Don't be so nice to me. I don't deserve it."

"Ah now, I disagree. If anyone deserves to be treated nice, it's you."

"Because my husband died?"

"Nope."

"Then, why?"

"'Cause I said so."

"You can't come up with a reason."

Jace could come up with plenty of reasons, but he knew if he said any of them out loud, she'd think he was crazy.

"I'm getting hungry."

"Me, too."

"Can we go inside now?"

"As soon as you and I agree to a truce. No more fightin'. We're on the same side, Bree. We both want the best for Blythe and her baby."

"Okay," she whispered. "Truce."

He kissed her forehead again. For a moment, he considered holding on a little longer. The idea of letting her go left him feeling emptier than it should.

Mark made linguine with clam sauce and had a bottle of wine open when they came inside.

"We didn't get very much moving done today," complained Lyric.

Blythe patted her hand. "We'll finish tomorrow. There's no hurry."

Jace and Bree moved away from each other and sat on opposite sides of the table.

Jace sat next to Blythe but couldn't take his eyes off Bree. How hard had the last few weeks been on her? It was as Blythe said. He wasn't mean to anyone, but he was always snapping at Bree. He was going to try not to lose his patience anymore.

His resolve was short-lived when, a few minutes later, Bree was talking to Blythe again about moving.

"We can go shopping tomorrow and pick out some things for the baby's room."

Jace tensed and was about to say something, when he felt Blythe's hand on his arm.

"That sounds nice, Bree. I'd like that."

"Can I come, too?" asked Lyric.

"Of course," answered Blythe. "We could pick up some more furniture for the rest of the house, too."

Jace kept quiet; he was clearly outnumbered. He wasn't sure how he was going to be much help with the baby if he wasn't living with her, but they had time to figure it out.

When he looked up from his bowl of pasta, Bree smiled at him. He smiled back. She won this round. That didn't mean she was going to take the title.

"I'll follow you back to the house and help you unload," he offered when dinner was finished.

"That's okay, we can handle it."

"Don't be stubborn, Bree. Let him help us," Lyric said.

"I'm gonna stay here tonight. Is that okay with everybody?" asked Blythe. "In fact, I'm going to call it a night now," Blythe yawned. "I've got a good book I'm in the middle of. Two or three pages in, and I'm sure I'll be sound asleep."

"What's it about?" Lyric asked.

"You know—cowboys, romance...that kind of stuff."

"My favorite! Can I read it when you're finished?"

"Of course." Blythe yawned again. "Good night, everybody."

Jace followed Bree to Palmer Lake. Forty-five minutes later, he had the boxes and clothes unloaded. "Do you want me to help unpack?"

"No, we can do that. Thank you so much for your help tonight."

"I should go," he said at the same time she asked if he wanted a beer.

"Okay," they both said, and then laughed.

"Beer?"

"Sure," he answered. "I'd love one."

Bree handed him a bottle, went into the living room, and sat on the sofa. Jace sat next to her and took a sip of his drink. "Interesting day."

"That's an understatement."

They sat in silence while he finished his beer and she drank a glass of wine.

"I should go," he said and stood.

"Right. Um, thanks again for your help today."

"Sure thing." He walked to the door and she followed. "See you tomorrow?"

"Sounds good."

He was about to walk out the door when she said his name.

"Yeah?" he turned around.

"I don't know how to thank you."

He leaned in and kissed her cheek. "No thanks necessary, darlin'."

"Mornin'," Jace said when Bree walked in her parents' kitchen.

"Where is everybody?"

"Out for breakfast."

"Why didn't you go?"

"I was waitin' for you." He was reading the newspaper and intentionally didn't look up when he spoke.

"Where are they? I'll go meet them."

"They'll be back soon. I'll make you somethin' if you're hungry."

"This is my—"

"Don't do it," he cautioned.

"What?"

"Don't say whatever it is you're thinkin'."

"What makes you think I'm thinking anything?"

When he stood and walked toward her, she walked in the opposite direction.

"Bree, you runnin' away from me?"

"No."

"What would you like for breakfast?"

"Nothing. And I should be asking you that question. We're in my parents' house."

He smiled, and she did too.

"How about some eggs?"

"Okay, I mean…"

"How do you like them, darlin'?"

"Whatever you make will be fine."

He went over to the refrigerator and pulled out eggs, some cheese, and vegetables. "How 'bout an omelet?"

"You don't have to—"

He held up his hand. "I want to."

"Why?"

He had no idea how to explain it, even to himself. He'd made a commitment to Blythe. She was his first priority, and even if she didn't love him now, he hoped she would someday. Yet, he found himself thinking about Bree just as much as her sister.

Granted he couldn't remember the last time he had sex, and Blythe being pregnant with his brother's baby didn't exactly stoke his fire. Maybe that was why Bree made him feel so…horny when she was near.

"What are you thinking about?"

"Huh? Nothing, why?"

"You have a funny look on your face."

"Somethin' I need to do, that I forgot about."

"Interesting."

"What?"

"The look on your face."

It wasn't his face he was worried about, it was another part of his body. If she noticed that, she'd know exactly what he'd been thinking about.

What made it worse, if that was possible, was he was thinking about sex with *her,* not just sex. What was wrong with him?

"Jace, are you okay?"

"Yeah, I'm fine. I gotta get somethin' out of my truck. Be right back." It wasn't something he needed to get, it was something he needed to get rid of, namely his raging hard-on.

He came back a few minutes later.

"What did you need to get?"

"Huh?"

"You said you had to get something out of your truck, but you didn't bring anything back in with you."

"Oh, right. I left it at Billy's. That's what took me so long; I was looking for it."

"What was it? If it's something important, maybe you could borrow it from my dad."

Just when he felt it coming back, he heard the garage door open, and Paige walked in. *Thank God.*

"Sorry we missed you, sweetie. How long have you been here? You could've come and joined us."

* * *

Sexual frustration. That's what Tucker felt when he woke up a little past noon. The weird part was, he had no desire to have sex.

The other thing he was feeling was the overpowering urge to talk to someone in his family. It didn't matter who, his mom, his dad, or his brother. Any of them. He missed them so much. If he contacted them, though, they'd try to talk him into coming back. And that was something he couldn't do.

15

Blythe was settled in her room, taking a nap. They hadn't gone shopping, but concentrated instead on getting everything unpacked. Paige and Mark came and helped, too. It was almost six o'clock before they finished.

"I didn't realize she had this much stuff," said Paige.

"When was the last time you were in her bedroom?" Bree asked.

"God knows."

"It was packed full of crap."

"Like your dad."

"Who's hungry?" Mark smiled.

"I am," answered Paige. "Are you cooking or buying?"

"Buying, definitely. I'm too tired to cook."

"Good. I want someone to bring me a nice glass of wine, a fabulous meal, and then clean everything up when I'm finished."

"Jace, will you join us?" Bree asked.

"Sounds good to me."

"How about you, Lyric? We're buying," added Mark.

"Should we check and see if Blythe wants to go with us?" Lyric asked.

"Yeah, or if she wants us to bring her back something." Jace and Bree both started toward her door.

"You go," she said.

"No, I'm sorry. Your house. You go."

When she came back out, she told them Blythe was sound asleep. Paige suggested they leave a note and tell her to call when she woke up, and they'd bring something back for her.

Jace was outside with Mark when Bree came out.

"What?" Bree asked when Jace looked at her.

"Nothing." It was a whole hell of a lot more than nothing, but he wouldn't tell her that.

Blythe woke in a cold sweat. Her stomach was cramping. She got up and made her way into the bathroom. Blood. *Oh, no. God, no.* She couldn't be losing the baby. Where was everybody? Why was she here alone?

When they came back from dinner, Bree went to check on Blythe.

"*Call an ambulance!*" she screamed.

Jace raced in, already calling 9-1-1. "*What happened?*" He stopped when he saw Blythe on the floor.

"Oh, God. No." He scooped her up and carried her out of the bathroom. He could hear the sirens already.

* * *

Tucker got a chill. Someone walked across his grave; that's what his grandmother would've said. He couldn't shake the feeling. There were only two other times in his life he'd felt this way. They were the worst two days of his life.

He didn't care what it cost him; he had to call Jace. Something was terribly wrong, and he had to find out what.

He pulled out his burner phone and punched in Jace's number. It rang and rang on the other end. Tucker tried again. After the fifth try, he left a message.

"It's Tuck. Call me." He left the number on Jace's voicemail and hung up.

* * *

The ambulance took Blythe to Memorial Hospital and straight into the emergency room. Paige and Mark were with her. Bree looked frightened, and Jace wished he could comfort her, but he was as frightened as she was. Every so often, their eyes met, but neither spoke.

Lyric was back and forth between the waiting room and outside. Jace pulled his phone out to check the time. Five missed calls and one message, all from a number he didn't recognize. He tried to slip the phone back into his pocket without Bree noticing. He'd wait a couple of minutes, until Lyric came back in, then he'd go out and listen to the message. He looked at Bree.

"Did you hear from him?"

"Maybe."

"Did he leave a message?"

"I think so."

"Listen to it."

He didn't know how Bree knew, but she did. He pulled the phone out and listened to the voice mail. It was Tucker all right, and he wanted him to call him back. What the hell was he going to tell him? He didn't know what was going on himself.

"What should I do, Bree?" he asked. The question slipped out.

"Call him, and tell him to get his fucking ass here as fast as he can."

"But what—"

"Call him, Jace. *Now.*"

Jace went outside. He couldn't talk to Tuck while Bree listened.

"Hey," Tuck answered.

"Where the fuck are you?"

"I'm nowhere."

"If I could, I'd reach through this phone and beat the shit out of you. Answer me—where the fuck are you?"

"It doesn't matter."

"You need to get your ass back here as soon as you can, no matter what it takes to make it happen."

"What's going on, Jace?"

He heard the desperation in his brother's voice. Where to start? "You're about to lose your baby, asshole." Jace hung up. There wasn't anything more he could say. It was up to Tuck now. He either came or he didn't.

"Well?" Bree asked when he walked back in.

"He's on his way. I think."

"You think?"

"It's up to him now, Bree."

"What did you tell him?"

"Enough." Jace prayed it was.

* * *

His baby? What was Jace talking about? He couldn't have a baby. He'd only been with Blythe since before Thanksgiving. Then the accident happened. *There couldn't be a baby.* Jace wouldn't fuck with him about something like this, though. If his brother said there was a baby, there had to be one. If there was a baby, Blythe was pregnant.

He left the bar. He didn't tell anyone he was leaving. He didn't go back to his room. He kept his ID and money strapped to his body. He couldn't afford to lose either, so he kept them on him at all times. There wasn't anything else in his room he would need.

When he got to the private airstrip, he found someone who agreed to fly him to the States, for the right price. Tucker reached in and gave the man twice what he'd asked for.

Five hours later, they landed on another private airstrip outside Colorado Springs. It was 3:00 AM, and there was a car waiting for him. Amazing what he could accomplish by throwing enough cash at it.

Tucker called Jace. "I'm here. Where are you?"

"Memorial Hospital." Jace hung up on him again.

Twenty minutes later, Tucker pulled up in front the emergency room and saw Jace outside, waiting for him.

"I'll park it. Go in there and beg them to tell you something. You'll have to tell them you're the baby's father."

He grasped the door and held on until he was sure he could put one foot in front of the other. He saw Bree and Lyric standing inside. Both looked as though they wanted to kill him. He understood how they felt—he wanted to kill himself more than both of them put together.

He watched as Bree walked over to the desk. She pointed at him.

"You're sure?" the nurse asked as he approached.

"Yes. I'm sure," Bree answered.

"Come with me." The nurse led him through the double doors.

Tucker closed his eyes, took a deep breath, and opened the door to Blythe's room when the nurse told him it was okay to go in.

The look on Paige and Mark's faces mirrored that of Bree and Lyric a few minutes before. Neither spoke to him. Paige walked out of the room.

"What's happening?" he asked Mark, praying Blythe's father would grant him the grace of telling him.

"We almost lost both of them tonight. But for now, they're both stable."

"Both?"

"Blythe and your baby, you *sonuvabitch*."

Tucker could feel the rage coming off of Mark as he walked past him and out the door.

He sat in a chair next to the bed and held Blythe's hand. It was cold. He looked her up and down, and laid his hand on the swell of her stomach. She looked at him, put her hand on top of his, and then closed her eyes again. He thought maybe she hadn't woken up completely. But no, he knew she had seen him when tears streaked her cheeks.

He didn't move for three hours. Periodically, someone would come in to check on her, but they didn't speak to him. They'd check her pulse and blood pressure, and then leave.

An hour later, Blythe woke up for the second time. "Why are you here?"

"Jace called me."

Jace called him? That meant Jace had known how to get in touch with him all along? Blythe felt as though her heart was being ripped out of her chest. Jace, the one she trusted, the one she believed in, had been lying to her.

"Get the hell out," she spat.

"Blythe, I'm so sorry—"

"Get. Out."

Monitors started beeping, and a nurse rushed in.

"Her blood pressure is spiking. You need to leave." Her voice was low and soft, but the way she said the words, she might as well have been screaming at him.

"What's going on?" Jace asked when Tucker came back out the double doors.

"Blood pressure. They wanted me to leave for a minute." Not exactly the truth, but he had every intention of going back in as soon as they'd let him.

"Have you talked?"

"Not very much."

Jace pulled his brother by the arm, away from Blythe's family.

"Talk. Now."

"She asked me why I was here, that's about it."

"And what did you say?"

"I told her you called me."

Jace's head was spinning. Tucker told her he'd called him? He hadn't called him, he called him back. Up until a few hours ago, Jace hadn't known how to reach him. He could only imagine what Blythe was thinking. She'd think he lied to her. That he'd betrayed her. He had to get in to see her, to explain.

When he approached the nurse in the waiting area and asked if he could go back, she asked him his name.

"No. I'm sorry. Ms. Cochran has left explicit instructions that neither Jace nor Tucker Rice be permitted in to see her."

"But—"

"If I'm forced to, I'll have security remove you from hospital property."

Jace noticed that Bree, the last person he wanted to overhear their conversation, had.

"What have you done?" Bree asked.

He took her arm to guide her away from Tucker, but she jerked it away. "If she's refusing to see you, there must be a good reason," her voice was venomous.

"It's a misunderstanding."

"Right." She turned to walk away, and Jace grabbed her arm again. When she spun around to face him, he was sure she was going to slap him. By the look on her face, she'd intended to, but stopped herself.

"She thinks I called Tucker. Which I did, but as you know, I called him back. There's a big difference."

"She thinks you knew where he was all along."

"Exactly."

"Did you?"

"Bree, you and I have had our differences, but if I had known where Tucker was, you know I would've said so."

She seemed skeptical, but the look of hatred that had been in her eyes moments before was gone. She was at least considering he was telling the truth.

"Bree Fox? Is there someone here named Bree Fox?" There was an orderly standing by the double doors leading back into the emergency room, calling her name.

"I'm Bree Fox," she answered, walking in his direction.

"Your sister would like you to come back."

"Please, Bree. Tell her. Please," Jace implored.

She met his eyes, but didn't answer.

"Are they still out there?" Blythe asked.

"Of course, they are, sweetie, and they aren't going anywhere."

"I've had it with the two of them. I don't want anything to do with either of them."

"Blythe, you know I am not Jace's biggest fan, quite honestly, I don't like him. But even I believe he's been telling the truth. If he'd known where Tucker was all this time, he would've said so."

"Bullshit. The two of them have been using me in a tug-of-war since the day I met them. Jace saw this as his opportunity to win me over. Tucker's gone, he's the hero. How can you not see through it? I can't believe he has you snowed."

"Tucker called him, and Jace called him back. I saw it unfold."

"Did you hear their conversation?"

Bree shook her head.

"It doesn't matter anyway. Tucker is back, so Jace is off the hook. It makes no difference that I don't intend to have anything to do with Tucker. His obligation to take care of his brother's cast-off and her bastard child are over."

"Blythe!" Bree gasped.

"What? I knew it was a game all along. My only mistake was having sex with one of them. I'll pay for that mistake for the rest of my life."

"You can't possibly think this baby is a mistake."

"Not the baby—the baby's father. We may be tied together by this child—that's if Tucker doesn't disappear again—but otherwise, I plan to have as little as possible to do with him or his family."

"What have they said about the bleeding?"

"They said I have partial placenta previa. Mom said she had it when she was pregnant with me. I don't understand it, but for now, I'm on bed rest."

"Will they let you go home at least?"

"I think so, but they're waiting to run more tests. I may have to have a blood transfusion."

16

Tucker went outside to wait. He couldn't stand being in the waiting area with Blythe's parents. He knew what they thought of him for leaving. He had his reasons, and seeing Blythe in that bed, knowing she and her baby were still at risk, made him want to catch the first plane right back out of there.

But he couldn't. This was something he couldn't run from, even if he believed they'd be better off without him. At the very least, he had to make Blythe understand why he'd left in the first place. If she'd listen, she might decide she didn't want him to stay. It had to be her decision. He wouldn't walk out on her and the baby unless he knew it was what she wanted.

When he saw Bree, Jace stood.

"Mom, she wants you and Dad to go back in now."

Paige and Mark went through the double doors without speaking to Jace, or even acknowledging he was still there.

"This isn't fair," he muttered. "Were you able to talk to her?"

"Yes, I talked to her, but I didn't get anywhere."

"You know I'm telling the truth. Or is this your way of getting rid of me?"

"How dare you accuse me of *anything*, especially lying to my sister?"

"Gotta admit, she'll believe whatever you tell her. You haven't made your feelings about me a secret."

"A moment ago, you said something about this not being fair, and right now, you aren't being fair to me. I'm not a liar, Jace. I may not like you, but I wouldn't lie to my sister to get rid of you."

He studied her, trying to figure out whether she was telling him the truth.

"What did she say?"

"Apologize."

"She said to apologize?"

"No. She didn't. Before you ask me what she said, you owe me an apology."

He hesitated, and Bree turned to walk away. "Wait. I'm sorry."

She turned back and studied him, much in the same way he'd been studying her moments before.

"I'm sorry, okay? I'm on edge. I'm beyond frustrated, but I shouldn't have accused you of lying."

"She doesn't believe me, but I did defend you."

"What was her response?"

"I told her that I saw it all take place. She asked me if I heard your conversation, and I had to tell her the truth. I didn't hear it."

"She believes I knew where Tucker was all along. Why would I have kept that from her? It doesn't make sense."

"To win."

Ah—Blythe believed it was still a game between the three of them. "That's crazy."

"I don't recommend you say that to her if you're given the opportunity."

"No. I wouldn't. But this is life, Bree. We're talking about a baby's life. And Blythe's life. I stepped in because Tucker wasn't here, because it was the right thing to do, not because I wanted to win a prize. What a low opinion she must have of me to think her life would mean so little."

Jace sat down and put his head in his hands. He'd done everything he knew to do for Blythe, yet she still believed he'd been lying to her, that it had only been a game.

He knew his feelings mattered little in this scenario, but it didn't change how hurt he felt. He'd offered Blythe his heart. Whether or not she could return his love, he'd been willing to give her his, and she still thought it was all a game to him. He wondered what that said about the kind of person people believed him to be. He'd spent almost every day of the last couple of months with her, yet she didn't know him at all.

"I'll talk to her again. I'll keep talking to her."

"Thank you, Bree. I know this isn't easy for you."

"It isn't about me. It's about her. And Tucker. And you. I'll tell her I believe you, but even if she accepts it, nothing much changes. With Tucker back in the picture, she won't need you in the same way. And she wants nothing to do with him either."

"It's his baby."

"She knows that. It doesn't mean she'll want him in her life. The baby's life, maybe. Her life, I don't know what to think."

"I'm going back upstairs now," she told him. "I just came down to tell you what she said."

"Thanks, Bree. I mean it sincerely."

She nodded and walked away, leaving Jace feeling as though there was a gaping hole in his chest. Was it because Blythe didn't believe him, or because he didn't want Bree to leave?

Blythe was being moved up to a room on the obstetrics floor since she'd be in the hospital at least overnight. The doctor explained the placenta previa meant part of the placenta was covering the opening of the cervix, which is why Blythe experienced bleeding. Since the placenta was only partially covering the opening, the doctor hoped that, as the uterus grew, the placenta would move higher, and the blockage would no longer be an issue.

If that happened naturally, Blythe would be able to resume normal activity. If it didn't, he would insist on bed rest for the remainder of the pregnancy.

"Bree?" Jace stood when he saw her get off the elevator again an hour later.

"I'm on my way to give blood."

"How is she?"

"She's being moved to a different floor so they can monitor her and the baby." She looked around him into the waiting area.

"Did Tucker leave again?" Bree asked him.

"No. He's outside."

"You might as well go home. I mean, not home, but wherever you're staying. Where are you staying?"

Jace had been staying with Billy and Renie. Now that Tucker was here, he didn't know. He was sure it would be okay, but he wouldn't want to impose. It might be better for them to get a hotel room close to the hospital.

"Is there any chance she'll talk to me?"

"Not yet, and honestly, Jace, there isn't any hurry. Why risk getting her worked up right now? Be patient. You'll get your chance to clear this up."

"Thanks. You're being awfully nice to me."

"Don't get used to it," she teased.

It was nice to see Bree smile. Nicer than he wanted to admit. What he wanted more than anything was to ask her to hug him. It sounded silly, even to him, but it had been too long since someone had.

As if she'd been beckoned, Lyric bounded up to them. "What's the word?"

Bree filled her in on Blythe's condition.

"Why aren't you with her? Or Tucker? I saw him sulking out front."

"She doesn't want to see them," Bree answered for him.

"Uh oh."

"Yep," answered Jace this time. "She thinks I've been lying to her."

"About what?"

"She thinks I knew where Tucker was."

"Did you?"

"No."

"Okay, then. Blythe will believe you when you tell her yourself."

Jace hoped she was right.

"Aren't you supposed to be in Pueblo?" she asked.

"Yeah, I called Billy, and he withdrew my name."

"What's next?"

"Crested Butte, to train."

"You gotta go, dude. Can't be sittin' around here. That was your agreement with Blythe."

"I'm not leaving until I straighten things out with her."

"Gotcha. So where are you and ol' brood-monster stayin'?"

"I asked him the same question." Bree sounded pissy again.

Lyric put her hand on her hip. "What did he say?"

Jace loved that Lyric handed Bree's pissiness right back to her. Although, right now he needed them both in his corner, which meant they couldn't be at odds with each other.

"We'll get a room somewhere nearby. Not a big deal."

"You can stay with us."

Jace thought Bree's eyes were going to pop out of her head.

"What?" Lyric saw Bree's look, too.

"They cannot stay with us, Lyric, and before you make an offer like that, you should consider asking your roommate her opinion."

"Oh jeez, Bree, lighten up. Don't know 'bout this one here, but the other one will be your brother-in-law someday. Maybe you should start bein' nicer to him."

"It's okay. A hotel will be easier, and closer."

"Maybe you oughta go stay with them, Bree, you'll be closer."

Jace anticipated that, any second, Bree would either storm off or tear into Lyric. But she didn't. She laughed. Lyric had a way about her that Bree responded to. Jace should ask her to give him lessons. The more he was around her, the more he wanted Bree to like him.

Blythe needed rest, so Paige and Mark talked every-one into leaving. Everyone but Jace and Tucker, who they didn't bother talking to.

Jace approached his brother, who was sitting on a bench by the hospital entrance. "Hey, man, let's go find a place to stay."

"I'm good."

"They're not gonna let you hang out on this bench all night. I've got some clothes at Billy and Irene's. I can swing by there, get 'em, and then we can get somethin' to eat."

"You go on ahead."

"Tucker, come on. She won't see you."

"Don't care. I'm not leavin'."

"First, you leave when you shouldn't. Now, you won't leave when you should."

"Shut it, Jace."

"She's sleeping. When's the last time you slept? Or ate?"

Tucker didn't remember, and he didn't care. He had to get back in to see Blythe. He had to tell her, make her understand. He left for her, to keep her safe. If he'd known she was pregnant, he might not have left. He couldn't say for sure.

"Go, do whatever you need to do. I'm staying."

"They won't let you in to see her."

"We'll see."

Irene was at the house when Jace got there. And she didn't look happy.

"What? And before you answer that, every woman I've come in contact with today has yelled at me. If you're gonna pile on more, save it. I guarantee you, I've already heard it."

Irene walked over to the oven and pulled out a plate wrapped in foil. She set it down on the counter in front of Jace.

"What's this?"

"Dinner."

"Uh, thanks."

Willow came running toward him, and waited for him to pick her up. When he did, she wrapped her little arms so tightly around his neck, he thought he'd choke.

"Thanks, baby girl," he said, pulling his head back a little ways from hers. "You don't know how much I needed that."

Willow didn't let go. He could swear she sensed his sadness and wanted to make him feel better.

Pretty soon she started babbling, but he could only make out every other word of what she was trying to tell him.

"Yes, baby girl. After your bath, you can try to talk Uncle Jace into reading you a story."

"How did you get all that?"

"You get used to it." She patted his hand. "You'll get used to it, too."

"I guess you haven't heard."

"I heard. Tucker's back, and Blythe isn't speaking to either of you."

"What else have you heard?"

"That's it, other than they're keeping her overnight. I'll go and see her in the morning."

"Is that why you're here instead of in Crested Butte?"

"Of course it is. She's my best friend, Jace."

He nodded.

"If it helps any, in the eighteen years Blythe and I have been friends, she's sworn she's never going to speak to me again at least once a year."

"I doubt whatever she was mad at you for, is anywhere near as serious as this, though."

"What Tucker did was serious, but nothing you did was. She's strung out. She'll listen to reason after she's gotten some rest."

"Will you help plead my case?"

"I heard Bree already did."

"You haven't missed much."

"Best friend, remember?"

"You think she'll realize she's wrong about me?"

"I do."

"Then there's the issue of Tucker." He shook his head. Much harder, but no less important. More important, in fact. "He's her baby's father."

"There's an easy solution."

"Oh yeah? What is it?"

"It starts with you and Tucker telling her the truth about what happened on Thanksgiving. Both Thanksgivings. Tell her why Tucker left the way he did and what happened that makes him act the way he does."

"He wants to tell her. In fact, I think he wanted to tell her before the accident. She told me they were on their way to 'talk' when it happened."

"And for some reason, he decided to leave rather than talk to her *after* the accident."

"He decided to leave *because* of the accident."

"This is getting tiresome, Jace. The two of you need to let go of this secret. It's ridiculous."

Maybe Tucker could tell his part of the story, but Jace wasn't sure he'd ever be able to talk about the role he played. Tucker didn't even know Jace's side of the story, and if he did, Tuck would never forgive him.

Irene walked over and rubbed his shoulders. "Jace, this isn't like you. Whatever it is, get it out. Talk about it."

"I wish I could."

"We should go for a ride. It worked for me."

Jace laughed. It had worked for her. The day he'd asked her to go for a ride and tell him everything she loved, and everything she didn't, about Billy Patterson, was the day they both realized how much she loved him. It was also the day Jace realized she'd never love him the way she loved Billy.

"This is different."

"It doesn't matter how it's different. It matters how it's the same."

"And how's that?"

"There's something going on with you that you're keeping inside, not talking about, maybe not even acknowledging your feelings about. That's the same."

Everything she said was true. He doubted very much he'd ever be able to talk to anyone about it. Not even her.

Blythe was asleep when Tucker crept into her room. The nurse had just left, which meant he had at least an hour before anyone came to check on her again.

He hated to wake her, but they had to talk. He had to talk anyway, and she had to listen. He sat and watched her sleep. It wasn't the first time he'd done this. The night they'd spent together, when they conceived the baby growing inside her, he'd watched her while she slept. She was as exhausted then as she was now. As strung out, too.

She hadn't had much of a break between then and now. Pain, surgeries, pregnancy, almost losing the baby and, above all else, worry. The whole time, she also worried about him. He knew it as well as he knew his own name.

There was another thing he knew. She loved him. She was angry, and hurt, but she loved him.

She'd listen to him when she was ready. He didn't need to do this tonight. He changed his mind about waking her. Instead, he'd let her sleep, get the rest she and the baby needed. He longed to rest his hand on the swell of her stomach, like he had when he first saw her. If he did that, though, she'd wake up.

For the last twelve hours, he'd been thinking about himself, not about her. He wanted to tell her, he wanted her to understand why he left, he wanted her to listen to him. But he hadn't stopped to consider what she wanted.

He imagined that when he was gone, she'd wanted him to be there for her, to hold her and comfort her, but he hadn't been here to do any of that.

"I love you, Blythe," he whispered. "I love you so much. I'm going to show you how much."

Tucker crept back out of the room as silently as he had come in.

Blythe had been holding her breath, waiting, waiting, waiting, to see what he'd do, what he'd say. He sat so quietly, for so long, she wasn't sure why he came in. She hadn't decided what she'd do if he tried to talk to her. She wanted to hear what he had to say. She prayed whatever it was would be enough that she could forgive him. That's what she wanted more than anything—to forgive him. She wouldn't make it easy on him, though. He didn't deserve for it to be easy.

He said he loved her. That was almost enough by itself for her to forgive him. But she knew that, if she let him off that easy now, eventually she'd have to get answers. By then, he might not be willing to give them.

She had to stand her ground. He had to tell her why he left, and what happened in his past that made him leave all the time. He also had to promise her he'd never leave again, and he had to be convincing enough, when he did, that she believed him.

When Tucker came out of Blythe's hospital room, Blythe's father was waiting for him.

"Thought you left."

"I'm back. Come with me," he said, motioning toward the elevator. "Please," he added when Tucker hesitated.

"Where are we going?"

"To the chapel. It's on the second floor."

"I'm not much of a praying man," Tucker admitted.

"You will be today."

There wasn't anyone in the chapel when they went in.

"Have a seat," Mark said, motioning to the pew. He walked around and sat in the pew in front of Tucker and rested his arm on the back of it.

"It's clear to me that there's more going on here than you being an asshole."

Tucker shook his head and looked at the ceiling. "Depends on how you look at it, I guess."

"Do you have anyone you can talk to?"

Did he? He had, all those years ago, but it hadn't helped. Would it help now? Doubtful. And even if he thought it would, he wouldn't know how to go about finding someone—assuming Mark was suggesting a shrink. "No," he finally answered.

"Son, it's obvious you care about my daughter. It's also obvious that something happened in your past that is keeping you from moving forward with your future."

"That about says it all."

"So the question is, what are you going to do about it? From where I sit, you have two choices. You can be in my daughter's life, and your child's life, or you can run again." Mark waited for Tucker to respond. When he didn't, he continued. "Whatever decision you make, it's gotta be one or the other. Blythe will not be able to handle you dropping in, and then dropping back out again."

Tucker put his head in this hands. "I don't know if I'm doing the right thing by staying."

"Tell me what I can do to help you."

Tucker sat up and looked at Mark. "I don't know. I don't even know how to help myself."

"That's an honest answer. I think the road to anything you want in life starts there. What if I found someone for you?"

"What do you mean? Somebody to talk to?"

Mark nodded his head.

Why not? He wasn't sure it would help, but wasn't Blythe worth the try? "Okay."

"Is there anything else you want to tell me before we head back?"

"I'm sorry I left. I honestly believed I was doing the right thing for everybody. I didn't know she was pregnant. If I had, I'd like to think I might've done things differently, but I can't say for sure."

"Another honest answer," Mark put his hand on Tucker's shoulder. "That's progress."

17

Tucker was still sitting outside, on that damned bench, when Jace came back. He didn't care what his brother said, it was almost eleven o'clock at night. He'd pick him up and throw him in the truck if he had to.

"Still keepin' the bench warm?"

"Nah. I'm ready to go."

"You are? Why didn't you call me?"

"I was enjoying the quiet a little longer."

"Did you try to see her?"

"I saw her."

"You did? Did she kick you out?"

"She was sleeping. I didn't want to wake her. There's time."

Jace was as confused as he was impressed with Tucker's attitude.

"Can we get something to eat?"

"Uh, sure. Irene fed me dinner at their place, but we can get you somethin'."

"Anything is fine. I don't care what. Then I need to sleep."

Jace drove across the street, where there was an all-night deli. He'd reserved a room in a hotel not far from the hospital. Tomorrow, he planned to try again to get Blythe to talk to him. Even if she wasn't ready to forgive Tucker, it was important to Jace that she know he hadn't lied to her.

Once they were in the room, Tucker fell asleep before Jace came out of the bathroom. Fully-clothed, boots still on, stretched out diagonally across the bed.

It took Jace longer. He hoped his brain was fried enough that he wouldn't dream tonight. He wanted to sleep like the dead, as long as his body would let him.

Blythe was finishing breakfast when Renie walked in the hospital room.

"Good morning!"

"Good morning to you, too. Where's that sweet little girl?"

"With your mom. She's practicing the grandma thing."

Blythe laughed. "I wonder if she'll let the baby call her grandma."

"Your mom will come up with something more unique."

Renie was right. Her mom would never settle for something as mundane as grandma. It would be as interesting to see what name she came up with for herself, as it would be to decide what to name her baby.

Oh God, she had to think of a name for the baby. Tucker should have some say in it, shouldn't he? And what would the baby's last name be? Would it be Cochran or Rice?

She hadn't thought about any of this while Tucker was gone. It was far too complicated. Had she gone the traditional route, like Brooke had, she'd be married already. Her husband wouldn't have left her for the first few months of her pregnancy, and she wouldn't have to worry about what the baby's last name would be. She hated to think Brooke was right about anything. But if she was here, Blythe would have to agree with her. Good thing she wasn't. Blythe laughed.

"What?" Renie asked.

"I was thinking about the lectures Brooke would be subjecting me to if she was here."

"Oh, gosh..." Renie started mimicking some of the things they both thought Brooke would be saying.

Bree arrived in the middle of it. "You two sound like Brooke," she said, which made them laugh harder.

"Renie, I wish you could stay closer to home. You're good for her," Bree told her.

"I won't be gone that long. I promised my mom I'd help when the baby's born, but as soon as I can, I'll come back. I promise."

"Sorry to put a damper on the mood in here, since it's so nice to see you having fun, but I've been asked to tell you the Rice brothers are downstairs."

"Ugh, no, don't be such a buzzkill."

"Tell me how you're feeling about them," said Bree.

Renie pulled a chair over, closer to the bed. "I talked to Jace last night."

"Yeah, and what did he say?"

"He didn't know where Tucker was. You have to know that. He wouldn't have lied to you. That isn't who he is."

"There's a part of me that knows that, or at least wants to believe it. I'm just so mad at both of them. Sometimes I wish I'd never met either one of them." Blythe stopped talking and rubbed her belly. "But if I hadn't met them, I wouldn't be having this baby, and right now, this baby is the most important person in the world to me."

Bree was crying.

"Don't cry, Bree! You're gonna make me cry. And I'm not sad. I'm mad. If I cry, I'll be pathetic. I want to be mean, and stubborn, and make Tucker Rice pay for…"

For what? For hurting her? Leaving?

"Do you want to see him?"

"I don't know. I do, and I don't. I'm mad, I'm not kidding about that. I'm hurt. And I'm scared."

"What are you afraid of, sweetie?" Bree asked the question, but Renie reached out and took Blythe's hand.

"That he won't want to stay."

"I don't think it's about want," Renie said. "The key is in getting him to talk about the big secret he and Jace share. Obviously, there was another accident. I'm guessing that whoever the girl was, died in it. We've all figured out that much."

"I would say you're right," added Bree. "But there's gotta be more to it."

"Get Tucker to talk, Blythe."

"What if he really loved her? What if he loved her more than he loves me? Maybe that's why he keeps leaving. What he wants is her, and he can't have her because she's dead. He thinks he wants me, but then when he's with me, I don't measure up."

"No, that isn't it at all. Not even close," a male voice said.

All three of them had been so focused on their conversation, they didn't hear the door open or Tucker walk in.

Renie released Blythe's hand and stood. Bree stood, too. They both looked at Blythe, who nodded her head.

"What is it, then?" Blythe asked him.

Tucker took a deep breath, and sat down in the chair Renie left empty.

Jace was pacing when Bree and Irene got off the elevator.

"Is he up there?"

"Uh, good morning, Jace. How are you?" joked Irene.

"Yes, he's up there," answered Bree.

"How is she?"

"Mad at him, but willing to listen."

"I hope he's willing to talk," added Irene.

Me too, thought Jace. Although Tucker wasn't the only one who needed to talk. He needed to tell his brother the role he'd played in what happened that night. And after he did, he wasn't sure he'd see Blythe, the baby, or any of these people again. If Tucker refused to forgive him, it would be Jace's turn to leave.

Irene's phone pinged, and she pulled it out of her pocket. *"Oh my God,"* she shouted. "My mom's water broke. I'm here, and my mom is having her baby. Shit. What am I going to do?"

"I'll drive you there," Jace offered.

"You're sure? I mean, should we drive? By the time I caught a flight, we could be there already. I'm so nervous. I have to pick up Willow. She's with Paige and Mark."

Jace chuckled. "Let's get on the road. The longer you stand here, the longer it will take us to get there."

"Tell Blythe, will you, Bree?"

"Of course—now, go!"

"Call your mom, and tell her we're on our way."

"I'll tell her to have Willow in the driveway, ready to go."

"Thanks! Oh my gosh, my mom is having a baby."

When they got to the hospital in Gunnison, her mother was still in labor. She hadn't missed it. "Do you mind?" she asked Jace, handing him Willow, and running toward the delivery room.

"Of course not," he answered, not that she could hear him; she was running as fast as she could.

"Okay, little girl, this is new for me. Let's see what we've got in here for you to play with."

Irene had two bags packed with stuff for Willow. She'd told Jace to leave one in the truck and bring the other one in. When Willow got tired, he could put her in the car seat, take her for a short drive, and she'd fall asleep. He laughed when she told him not to leave her in the car alone, and if they sat in the parking lot while she slept, to make sure it didn't get too warm.

"She doesn't have too much faith in my babysitting abilities, but we're gonna be fine, aren't we, Willow?"

Willow smiled and started babbling. She wanted him to read her a story; he understood almost all her words this time. He was making progress, or maybe she was.

Three hours and many snacks later, Willow screeched when she saw Irene walking toward them. "Mama mama!" she yelled and held her arms out.

"Well?"

Irene was smiling from ear to ear. "As she predicted, she had a little girl. She's beautiful, Jace." Irene had tears in her eyes. "I need to call Billy."

"Right here, sweet girl," Billy walked in as if on cue, and Irene threw her arms around him.

"Sorry I didn't get here sooner."

"It's okay."

"Mama cryin'," Willow explained to Jace. "Mama happy dada's here now."

"Glad to see you were able to keep our baby alive, Rice."

Irene slugged him. "Leave him alone. He did great." She looked at Jace. "Thank you, I don't know what I would've done without you."

"My pleasure, and I mean that sincerely." Jace ruffled Willow's hair. "We had fun, didn't we, Willow?"

Willow looked at Irene. "Had fun, Mama."

"Hey, what's her name?" asked Billy.

"Caden Avery," Irene told them.

"Ah now, isn't that a pretty name?"

"I should call Paige and Mark. And who else? There must be other people I'm supposed to call."

"Didn't she give ya a list?" Billy asked.

"You're right, she did. What would I do without you, Billy Patterson?"

"You ain't never findin' out, darlin'." He kissed her long and hard enough that it made Willow giggle and Jace blush.

Tucker wished Blythe's gaze wasn't quite so penetrating.

"I'm waiting," she said.

"I know you are. This isn't a story I've told before, Blythe. I'm trying to figure out where to start."

"Start at the beginning."

The beginning. That would've been all the way back to elementary school. The day the teacher announced to the class there was a new girl who would be joining them.

* * *

Her name was Rosa, and she was the prettiest thing he'd ever seen. Her last name was Rodriguez, which meant she'd be sitting right behind Tucker, since his last name was Rice. Jace sat in front of him.

He learned, over time, that Rosa's family lived in Basalt, but since her mother drove into Aspen for work every day, they enrolled her in a school in town. Rosa never believed she fit in with the other students, who primarily came from wealthy families. Her mother worked for one such family, as a housekeeper. It wasn't until they were freshmen in high school that Rosa began coming out of her shell, and that was after going to school with most of them for several years.

She was often off on her own, and Tucker watched her. He was the same way, sometimes anyway. There were days when he didn't feel like hanging out with his friends, he wanted to get lost in his art instead. There wasn't anyone he liked to draw more than Rosa. Her black hair and almost black eyes were such a contrast against her pale skin that flushed a pretty shade of pink whenever he talked to her.

"I want you to call me Rose," she said to him one day.

"Why?"

"I don't like Rosa. It's too...ethnic."

"But, it's you," he said. He ran his finger over her cheek when he said it, and she leaned her head into his hand.

"Rosa—beautiful Rosa. Please don't try to change who you are. You're perfect."

She blushed again, and that was the first time he kissed her.

Her parents were very strict, and were opposed to her dating a boy from Aspen, but Tucker was relentless. He made excuses to come and see her in Basalt on the weekends. He sketched her all the time, and for Christmas, he gave her parents a portrait he'd painted of her. They accepted him after that, and while they were still very strict with her curfew, they did allow her to go out with him.

Rosa's brothers didn't like Tucker or Jace. They'd gone to school in Basalt and worked the ski area. Both Tucker and Jace were on the ski team, so they ran into them often. The day Tucker tried to start a conversation with one of them, he'd told him and Jace to leave his sister alone.

Tucker didn't understand what he meant. Why had he said *they* should leave her alone?

"She's got a mind of her own," Jace said that day. Tucker pulled Jace away when it looked like a fight was brewing between him and Rosa's oldest brother.

Jace's reaction surprised him, and they argued. Tucker told him he could fight his own battles, and he didn't need Jace to intervene. It was important to Tucker that Rosa's family liked him, welcomed him, and accepted him.

It was one of the worst fights the two brothers had. Tucker could feel Jace's anger, and he didn't understand it. It didn't make sense to him.

When they were in their senior year of high school, Tucker approached his father the night before Thanksgiving. He wanted to propose to Rosa on Christmas Day and wanted to marry her right after graduation. His father wasn't opposed to Rosa, he told him. He liked her, but Tucker was too young to be married. His parents were in agreement that he should finish college before he thought about marriage. If he and Rosa still wanted to be wed then, they'd have his parents' support.

Tucker was invited to Rosa's house for Thanksgiving, and he went, hoping to have a chance to talk to Rosa's father. If he agreed to let them marry, maybe he could get his parents to change their minds.

Rosa's family was more against the marriage than Tucker's parents. Her father told Tucker it would never work between them. They came from two different worlds. Once Tucker went away to college, he'd see that more clearly. Rosa would never fit in his world. Tucker insisted her father was wrong. The economic differences in their families didn't matter, but her father was intransigent. He refused to discuss it further and asked Tucker to leave.

He was angry and didn't want to upset Rosa, so he left. On his way to the truck, he saw one of her brothers standing not too far from it. He ignored him. With the mood he was in, getting into an argument would just escalate things.

"*Cabrón,*" her brother said when he walked by. "Telling my father you want to marry my sister. You think Rosa loves you?"

Tucker kept walking.

"You think you're the only *pendejo* who comes around to see her? You're wrong, and you're the same— assholes, both of you."

Tucker knew Rosa's brother was trying to rile him, but he kept walking. When he got in his truck, he threw it into gear and drove away, his tires laying rubber on the road.

He drove and drove that afternoon. He went up to Independence Pass and hiked to the top. He sat there, trying to get his temper under control, until the sun began to set.

He drove back to Basalt then, hoping to talk to Rosa. He needed to see her.

When he pulled into the driveway, he saw two figures standing near the back shed. It looked like a man and a woman, in a heated embrace. He stopped the truck and climbed out, startling them. He heard Rosa gasp and realized she was with another man. She ran toward him, calling his name. He remembered backing away, turning, and getting in his truck.

"Wait," she screamed at him. She reached the passenger door before he could lock it, and climbed inside.

"Tucker, please," she begged. "Let me explain."

"Get out of the fucking truck, Rosa," he'd screamed at her.

She refused. "We have to talk," she told him. "You don't understand…I love him."

Tucker couldn't think straight. How could Rosa love someone else?

He told her again to get out of the truck. He looked up and saw the man walking out of the shadow of the darkness. If the man got any closer, Tucker was afraid he'd kill him.

"Get out of the truck, Rosa," he screamed at her. "If you don't, I'm leaving with you in it."

"Do it, then," she screamed back at him.

Tucker backed the truck out of the driveway and sped away. He didn't look back, he didn't see who the other man was.

"Tucker, I didn't mean for this to happen."

He didn't want to listen. She was ripping his heart right out of his chest. He drove faster and faster on the winding mountain road.

He was going around a curve when she pulled at his arm. He lost control of the truck. It barreled off the road and rolled. He remembered Rosa's terror-filled eyes boring into his.

***

"I looked at her, Blythe, right before the truck rolled. The look in her eyes…I'll never forget. She looked at me like I was supposed to save her, and I couldn't.

"She didn't live, Blythe. And it was my fault. Do you understand? It was my fault. I killed her that night, the only woman I ever loved. Until you."

Blythe nodded. "Go on, Tucker."

"I had internal injuries that required emergency surgery, and I ended up in the hospital for several days. Her family came to visit one night, but waited until my parents left before they came in the room. Her father was in a rage. That I could deal with, but her mother— her rage was far worse. The things she said to me…I'll never forget them."

"What did she say?" Blythe whispered.

"She cursed me. Screamed that I would never know love, because I didn't deserve it. She told me that even Rosa didn't love me, but she'd been too afraid to tell me. I didn't understand. Rosa never acted as though she was afraid of me. I was confused and heartbroken.

"Her mother told me Rosa had wanted to get away from me for months, but she was afraid of what I'd do when I found out she was in love with someone else. And then she told me Rosa loved someone close to me and knew, if she told me, *I'd kill him.*"

There were tears on Tucker's cheeks, and the final words he said came out as a sob. "I guess she was right, because when I saw her with another man, I did want to kill him. I honestly did. And that's why I wanted to leave, because I was afraid of that kind of rage. I wouldn't have hurt her, but I might have hurt him, whoever he was."

Blythe reached out her hand to him. He wanted to take it, he wanted to let her hold him, but he needed to finish.

"When I got out of the hospital, I lashed out at all of my friends. I knew it had to be one of them. I accused them all and swore them off. I never wanted to talk to any of them again. The only one I didn't was Chris, who you met at the restaurant. He and his wife, Kate, have been together since high school. Kate told me that Chris had been with her that night, and I knew she wouldn't lie about it. If she thought Chris had been unfaithful to her, she would've been in as much of a rage as I was."

"That's why you're such close friends."

"He was the only one I trusted. And Jace. They became the only people I'd talk to, other than my parents. Every man I saw, I wondered if he was with her that night. If he was the man she fell in love with."

After graduation, which he didn't attend, he left for Europe. He went to art school in Spain and decided to make his home there. He came back to the States for holidays but was always anxious to leave again. When he was in Aspen, he only saw his family, and occasionally Chris and Kate. Then he'd return to Europe.

It wasn't long before his work became known and US galleries were clamoring to represent him. In the last couple of years, he'd been coming back more often, but he still had no desire to live here again.

"Jace and I have a condo in Aspen, but I'm never there. It has my art in it, the pieces I've given to Jace, or the ones I haven't wanted to sell. In the last three years, I don't think I've slept there more than a dozen times."

"Spain is your escape."

"It has been."

"Is that where you were?"

"No, it isn't. I would've been too easy to find. I went to Mexico."

Blythe was taking it all in. He could see her processing the story he was telling her.

"When I came back before Thanksgiving, I had been feeling as though my life was meaningless. I wanted love, the kind of love my parents have—the kind that, since Rosa died, I never believed I could have—but I knew it was too much to hope for.

"And then there you were, with your violet eyes and obstinate attitude. The minute I saw you, I wanted you, and somehow I knew it wouldn't be meaningless between us. I could feel you. Our connection was immediate, and I know you felt it, too."

Tucker moved his chair closer to the bed. He wanted to hold her, but he wasn't finished.

"I didn't plan to leave on Thanksgiving. I didn't want to leave. I wanted to get away, push Rosa out of my head, and come back to you. Once I started driving, I kept going. Leaving is what I knew, what I know. Up until this last time, I always ran to Spain."

He told her he'd painted her every day when he was in Spain. He'd been with her less than twenty-four hours, but he could still remember everything about her. He told her he painted her hands, the curve of her spine, her smile.

"They're all in my house in San Sebastian. It's a seaside village on the Bay of Biscay, in Northern Spain, very close to the border of France."

He inched closer still, taking both her hands in his. "When Jace told me he planned to see you in January, I knew I had to come back. You are the first woman I've felt anything for since Rosa. For a while, I didn't think I would ever feel anything again, especially love. I didn't think it was possible."

He stood and she moved over so there was room for him. He gently climbed in and put his arm around her, bringing her closer to him.

"When Bree's husband died, I saw how you took on all her pain. You swallowed it and carried it for her. Whatever Bree was going through, you felt. I worried that if I told you my story, you would do the same with me. I wanted to tell you, but it was too soon. The funeral was that same day. It would have been selfish for me to burden you with my pain—my damage, as Jace calls it. But I knew, if there was going to be anything more between us, I needed to tell you."

He was torn, he told her, which was why he'd acted the way he did. He'd wanted to go to Aspen, to think, but he was afraid that if he did, he'd head right back to Spain. Then, the worst thing he could ever imagine happened.

"The accident," she whispered.

"I woke up. I saw you. Your back was to me, and I couldn't tell if you were breathing or not. The next thing I knew, I was in a hospital bed. *Again.*

"Rosa's mother's words came screaming back at me. She told me I'd never know love because I didn't deserve it. You know, I've never told anyone else what she said to me that night. I never told my parents or Jace that Rosa's parents came to see me in the hospital."

That was why Jace didn't understand, why no one understood. They thought he couldn't let go of Rosa, but that wasn't it. It wasn't about letting go, it was about believing in the future. That was the part he couldn't let himself do.

"You have no idea how hard it is for me to believe it now. Every part of me is terrified that if I'm in your life, something will happen to you or the baby.

"That's why I left. I believed you were better off without me. A couple of nights ago, when they brought you here, I knew something was terribly wrong. I couldn't stop myself from calling Jace. I had to know what had happened. The only other two times in my life I felt that way were when Rosa looked at me, right before the accident, and again, when you did."

Blythe shifted so she could get her arm further around him, hold him tighter.

"All Jace said was that I needed to get here, as fast as I could, because I was about to lose my baby. What that did to me, Blythe…I can't even describe how I felt. Hope mixed with the worst kind of fear I could imagine. If something happened to our baby because of me, I don't think I would've been able to go on. I still feel that way."

Blythe looked up at him.

"What is it? Ask me, tell me. Whatever it is, I can take it. Even if you say you don't want me here. I can take it, Blythe."

"You have to trust me, Tucker."

He wanted to believe it was that simple. He wanted to let himself love her—but the risk. That was what he struggled with. If he left now, and stayed out of their lives, she'd be okay. She'd raise the baby, find love, and live a full and wonderful life. If he stayed, he didn't know what might happen.

"I don't see it that way," she said. "I see a man who loved someone very much, who was hurt to his core, and then there was a terrible accident. That's what it was, Tucker. An accident."

He shook his head, but Blythe put her fingers to his mouth to quiet him.

"What about Rosa? She was with another man. She *loved* another man. How was that your doing? Whatever she believed, or told her parents she believed, was born of her own guilt, not of who you are. You're not a violent man. You are deep, and complex, and mysterious—but you're not violent.

"You're right; I felt you immediately, Tucker. If you'd told me this story that first night, when we had dinner, I would've said the same thing. I would've told you then that I didn't believe you had that kind of anger inside you."

"I don't know—"

"I do."

"How can you be so sure?"

Blythe reached for his hand. "Feel him," she said, bringing his hand to where hers rested on their baby. "You made him, and he's perfect. He's everything that's good in this world."

"Him?"

She kissed the tears rolling down his cheeks. "He's here to prove that you're wrong about yourself."

"What if I'm not wrong? What if—"

"No, Tucker, there are no 'what ifs.' You have to trust us."

"What if I can't take care of you? What if something happens to you because of me?"

"Tucker, listen to me. You have to believe in us. It isn't all up to you. We'll take care of each other."

Jace felt it. He knew Tucker told Blythe about Rosa. He was driving back from Crested Butte when it hit him. Now it was his turn. He had his own story to tell, and it would likely rip their lives to shreds.

18

Jace pulled in the driveway and saw Bree sitting on the front porch, reading a book. He didn't know why he came here, and he didn't know who he expected to find when he did. Was he looking for Lyric? Or Bree?

There was something that told him Lyric would go easy on him. If he told her the story, she wouldn't judge him. Maybe he was a fool for thinking so.

"Hey, there," he said as he got out of his truck. "Gettin' a little cold for you to be sittin' out here, isn't it?"

"I got caught up in my book, I guess. I didn't realize how late it was getting."

He walked up to where she was on the porch, and she stood. "Where's Lyric?"

"She had some family stuff to take care of but asked me to let her know if she was needed here, and she'd come back."

"Goin' inside now?"

"Yeah, I think I will."

He walked her to the front door and held it open.

"Uh, do you want to come in?"

"I would."

Bree dropped her book on the island in the kitchen and opened the refrigerator door. "We don't have much to eat. I could make you a sandwich."

"Nah, thanks. I'm not hungry."

"Somethin' to drink?"

"A beer would be nice if you've got one."

She pulled one out and handed it to him. She poured herself a glass of wine and followed him into the living room. She started to sit in one of the chairs, when Jace motioned her over and patted the seat on the couch, next to him.

"Come over here and sit next to me."

"Jace—"

"Bree, come and sit down."

When Jace woke up later, he had no idea what time it was. Bree was out cold on the couch, next to him. He eased himself out from under her, reached down, and picked her up. She felt as though she didn't weigh a thing as he carried her into the bedroom and laid her on the unmade bed. When he pulled the covers over her, she stirred.

"Don't go," she murmured. He wondered if she knew she said it, or if she was dreaming. He stood to leave, and she touched his hand. "Jace, please, don't go."

He toed off his boots and stretched out next to her. She moved closer and rested her head in the crook of his arm. He held her close, and they both fell back to sleep.

Jace opened his eyes and looked at the clock. It was a little after five in the morning. His arm was asleep, where Bree's head rested on it. They'd fallen asleep that way, and neither had moved.

Bree felt so warm against him, in contrast to the coldness he felt building in his chest. Something was wrong, and as much as he wanted to stay huddled in her warmth and ignore it, he knew he couldn't.

He eased his arm out from under her and rolled off of the bed. He hated to leave her, but the feeling of dread was not going away. If something had happened to Blythe or the baby, he needed to know. He prayed that wasn't it.

Jace took the back way from Palmer Lake to Mount Herman Road. He didn't know where he was going. He just kept driving southwest, toward the mountain.

It wasn't long after the road turned to gravel that he saw another truck. He pulled up behind it and parked. This was the site of Tucker and Blythe's accident. He could still see the scars it had left on the hillside.

As he climbed out, he saw Tucker farther up the hill. Jace made his way up the rocky terrain to where his brother sat on a big rock, his head in his hands.

"Tucker," he said. "I'm here."

Tucker looked up but didn't speak. He didn't need to; Jace could feel his anguish. He sat down next to him and waited.

It wasn't long before Tucker spoke. "She asked me to trust her," he said. "I want to, but I don't know how to let myself."

"Let go, Tuck. Quit holding on so tight to something that isn't there anymore."

"I don't know if I ever loved Rosa, or if it's turned into something so much bigger than it really was."

"I don't know."

"You don't remember?"

"I remember."

"Then how can you say you don't know?"

"I wasn't sure."

"What do you mean?"

"I wasn't sure if it was your feelings or my own."

"What are you talking about?"

"Tucker—"

"*Fuck.*"

After all these years, the truth about that night was finally working its way to the surface.

Tucker walked toward his truck. He wasn't sure he could drive, but he knew he couldn't stay here with Jace. The pieces were falling into place, and when they finished landing, he didn't want Jace anywhere near him.

"Tucker, wait."

He couldn't wait.

"Don't leave. Let's talk about this."

Talk about it? Was he kidding? Talk about it now? Seven years. That's how long it had been, and Jace wanted to talk about it now? No, they wouldn't be talking about it.

Tucker had the truck turned around and was about to head back down the mountain when Jace stepped in front of it.

He stopped, opened the driver's door, walked to where his brother stood, and swung with everything he had in him. When his fist connected with Jace's jaw, his brother fell backward. Tucker grabbed his shirt, steadied him, drew back, and hit him again. This time he was sure he'd broken Jace's nose.

He went to grab him again but made the mistake of looking in his brother's eyes. He couldn't stand what he saw in them.

"Get the fuck out of my way, Jace, or I'll run you over."

He walked back to the truck, put it in gear, and pulled forward. Jace was standing near his own truck, trying to stop the blood flowing out of his nose. Tucker kept driving.

Blythe gasped when he walked into the room. "Tucker...is everything okay?"

"No. It isn't."

He ran his hand through his hair and streaked blood through it when he did.

"Your hand is bleeding."

He looked at his knuckles. "It's nothing. It's fine."

When Blythe reached her hand out to him, he walked over to her.

"How can you keep doing this?"

"What?" she asked.

"Reaching your hand out to me."

"I'll never stop."

"Why not?"

"Tucker, how can you not know?"

He knew, but he needed to hear her say the words. "Tell me," he said.

She pulled him closer. "Tucker, the reason I won't ever stop is because I love you. When you love someone, you never stop reaching out to them."

Jace never felt so lost. All these years, he'd hoped Tucker would move on from that night, find a way to get over it. He should have known he wouldn't. At first, Jace had waited to tell him until he was out of the hospital. He told himself it would be easier after some time passed.

Each time he decided to tell him the truth, he found another excuse to put it off. He put it off so many times that it got to the point where he couldn't explain to Tucker why.

He should have a doctor check out his broken nose, but he didn't know where to go. There was only one person he could think of to call who he figured wouldn't make him answer any questions. He'd seen her car in the driveway when he left the house in the glen an hour ago.

"Hey, it's Jace," he said when Lyric answered. "Sorry to call so early."

"It's okay, I'm up. You don't sound too good."

"That's why I'm calling. I think my nose is broken."

"Oh my 'lanta! What happened? You practicin' at six in the morning or somethin'?"

"Nah. This had nothin' to do with a horse."

"That doesn't sound good either. Where you at?"

"It might be better if I came to you. Are you still at the house?"

"Yep, but how did you know that?"

"I saw your car when I left."

"When you left where? Here? I gotta hear this story. You and Bree? I coulda predicted that one. Damn, did I ever hook up with the right folks. Followin' along with all your drama makes my life look like a walk in the park."

"Lyric?"

"Yeah?

"My nose..."

"Right, right. Sorry. Meet me at the Speed Zone. You know where that is?"

He did. It was a coffee place only a couple of doors down from O'Malley's, right on the main drag.

"I'll be waiting out front," Lyric said before she disconnected the call.

"Holy smokes!" she said when she saw Jace. "You aren't kidding; your nose is broken. Jeez! What's the other guy look like?"

"Not a scratch on him, except maybe where his hand connected with my face."

"We gotta get you to an emergency room."

"Is there another hospital, other than the one Blythe is in?"

"I think so, but why? Wait, you know what? Never mind, forget I asked. Get in the truck, and I'll see if I can figure out the next closest."

Jace wanted to thank her, but it hurt so much to talk. "Thanks," he managed anyway.

"You got it. I tell ya, someday I am gonna write a book about you crazy Rice boys, might even throw Patterson into the story."

"Not funny."

"Wasn't tryin' to be. I am gonna write a book. You guys are too good of characters to pass up. Mark my words, it'll be a runaway best seller."

"Where do you want me to take you?" Lyric asked Jace when he came back through the door to where she sat in the waiting room. He didn't feel much better than he had when he'd gone in. In fact, he felt worse.

"Back to my truck."

"Sure you can drive?"

"No. Probably not."

"Are Billy and Renie at the ranch, or are they in Crested Butte?"

"They're in Crested Butte. Liv had the baby yesterday, or was it the day before. I have no idea, days are kinda runnin' together on me."

"You have a key?"

"Nope, but I know where they keep it."

"Think they'd mind if you crashed there?"

They already thought he was staying there, but last night he'd fallen asleep on the couch with Bree. He wished now he hadn't left her this morning. But Tuck had needed him, and he had to go to him, even if it meant his secret was now exposed.

He may have severed his relationship with his brother forever, but by doing so, he may have finally given Tucker what he needed to move on with his life. If he did that, he'd be able to be with Blythe and his baby, like he should be.

"You wanna talk about it?"

Did he? No, he didn't want to, but he needed to.

"Guess I better."

Lyric pulled out the bottle of Jack from where Irene and Billy kept it, and set it on the kitchen counter in front of Jace.

"How you feelin'?"

"Been better. Although it's been a long time since I have."

"Let's hear it."

Jace took a deep breath. He'd never told a living soul the story he was about to tell Lyric. He'd buried the words so deep, he wondered if he could pull them out of where he kept them hidden.

"When Tuck and I were in high school…" he began.

"We're going to let you go home, Blythe, but understand, you'll be on bed rest. If you don't take it seriously, we'll see you back here."

"I understand."

The doctor looked at Tucker. "Will you be the one taking care of her?"

Would he? He assumed so, but where? He had a lot to figure out, and he needed to do it in a hurry.

"We can stay with my parents," Blythe reassured him.

"For now."

"You should call them, Tucker, and let them know."

"Right, right. I'll call them."

Blythe wanted to giggle at how flustered Tucker was. She'd never seen him this way. And it didn't have anything to do with what had happened earlier. He was flustered about her, and their baby. She watched him until he finally looked at her.

"Nervous?" she smiled.

"Terrified might be a better word," he smiled back, but then his expression turned serious. "I don't want anything to happen to you, Blythe. I couldn't stand it if something did."

"Nothing will." She took his hand. "I promise."

19

"Are you sure this is okay?" he asked Blythe when they pulled in the driveway of her parents' house.

"It'll be fine, Tucker."

"I could try to rent a place, but we'd have to furnish it, and—"

"Tucker, relax. We don't have to figure everything out today. My mom and dad have plenty of room. It'll help, too, having my mom close by."

"You'll stay downstairs," Paige told them. "You'll have it to yourselves, unless you need us."

Her parents' house had three floors, as many of the homes in that part of Colorado did. Upstairs, there were four bedrooms and a loft that Paige used as an office. On the main floor, there was a large kitchen with an eat-in area. It was big enough to seat fourteen people at a long table made of reclaimed barn wood. There was also a formal dining room, a living room, music room, and a guest room.

On the lower level, there were three more bedrooms, a family room, another smaller kitchen, and Mark's recording studio. There were sliding glass doors off the family room that led directly outside where there was a hot tub. She and Tucker would have plenty of privacy downstairs as long as they wanted to stay.

"Tucker, where's Jace?" she asked once they were settled.

"I have no idea."

"What was the fight about."

"I don't want to talk about it, Blythe. I'm sorry, but I just can't yet."

"Was it about me?"

Tucker leaned over and kissed her forehead. "No, sweetheart, it wasn't about you."

Blythe couldn't imagine what it could have been about if not her. She'd let it go for now, but she wouldn't be able to stand the two of them being at odds if she could do anything about it. Jace had been her rock over the last couple of months.

"Can I get either one of you something to eat?" Paige called down from upstairs.

"I'm starving, Mom."

Paige walked halfway down the staircase. "How about you, Tucker?"

Tucker's stomach rumbled at the mention of food. "I am pretty hungry, now that you mention it."

"You got a bag or something?" Mark asked, standing on the step above Paige.

"What?" Tucker asked.

"You know, clothes, that kind of stuff?"

"I left where I was in a big hurry, so…"

"Jace got some stuff you could borrow?"

"Nah," he said, shaking his head. "I'll go out later and pick up some stuff of my own."

"I'll go see if I can find something you can change into in the meantime," Mark offered. "You're kinda starting to smell."

Her mom and dad left, each on a different mission.

"Come here," Blythe patted the bed next to her.

"I'm more nervous now than I was at the hospital, Blythe. I don't want to do anything to hurt you."

"Then get over here and hold me. If you don't, you'll hurt me more."

"Wow," Lyric rested her elbows on the counter in front of her and put her head in her hands.

Maybe he'd been wrong to tell her. Maybe she was judging him. He wished she'd say something other than *wow.*

She stood up and put her hands on his shoulders. "I gotta tell ya, as bad as this seems to you, and as bad as it seems to Tucker, it's something you have to talk about, and get it over with. Rosa wasn't who Tucker thought she was, and he needs to know that."

"I'm not who he thought I was either."

"Gotta say, you were a shit, but come on, you were what? Seventeen, eighteen?

Jace let out a huge breath. He hadn't realized how long he'd been holding it.

"I'm not sure he'll ever forgive me."

"He will, Jace. Maybe not as quickly as you want him to, but he will."

"They're at Paige and Mark's. Paige said they both fell asleep about a half hour after they got there," Lyric told Jace after she got off the phone.

"How's Blythe?"

"Good. She'll be on bed rest for a while."

"Did she say anything else?"

"She said the two of them seemed happy. Peaceful. Oh, and she told us to stop over later if we wanted to. I didn't say one way or another."

"She knows we're together?"

"Jace, it isn't that unusual. We've all been spending time together lately. It might not be a good idea for you to see Tucker until he's ready, but everything isn't a conspiracy, ya know."

"Was Bree there?"

"Ya know, she didn't say and I didn't ask."

"Someone should call her."

"I will."

She was on the phone for a minute and then disconnected the call. "It went straight to voicemail," she told him.

Jace wanted to tell Bree the story about Rosa himself. He didn't want her to hear it from Tucker or from Blythe. He didn't know why it was important that he be the one to tell her, but it was. After he did, he'd leave. There was no reason for him to stick around.

Billy was expecting him to start training in Crested Butte before rodeo season heated up. If he planned to make any progress as a competitive saddle bronc rider, he had to get out on the circuit.

"I'm starving," Lyric said.

"Me, too. What time is it anyway?"

"After two. Mind if I go and get somethin'?"

"How bad do I look?"

Lyric motioned for Jace to move his hand away from his face. "The swelling's gone down a lot, but you're still black and blue. You look good enough to go with me, if you want."

Jace couldn't sit still, and he didn't feel like drinking anymore. If Tucker wanted to talk to him, he didn't want his brother thinking he had gotten drunk because he was feeling sorry for himself.

"Yeah, I'll go with you."

Jace saw Bree sitting alone at a table when he and Lyric walked into the restaurant. He touched Lyric's arm and motioned in Bree's direction.

"Hey, there, can we join you?" Lyric asked in her typical upbeat way.

"Uh, sure."

"Hey," said Jace.

"Hi."

Lyric excused herself after they ordered a beer. "Be right back," she winked.

"Where does she always go?" Bree asked.

"I don't know. Listen, I wanted to talk to you. This isn't easy." He ran his hand over his face.

Bree stood and threw a twenty-dollar bill on the table. "Look, I know you're in love with my sister. You don't need to confess it to me. We can go back to not wanting to be in each other's company, starting now."

"Wait, where is this coming from?"

The pain meds, combined with the alcohol he'd consumed at Billy's impaired his reflexes. Bree was gone before Jace realized what was happening.

"What happened?" Lyric asked when she came back to the table. "I saw Bree pulling out of the parking lot. Is Blythe okay?"

Jace's head was still spinning. "I'm not sure what happened."

"Why'd she leave?"

"I don't know. She said something about me bein' in love with her sister and not wanting to be around me."

"She's got it bad."

"Who's got it bad?"

"Bree."

"What the hell are you talkin' about?"

"C'mon now, Jace. She's crazy about you. Open your damn eyes."

"How's your mom?" Blythe asked Renie when she called.

"Better than Ben," she laughed. "He's a nervous wreck. Keeps saying he doesn't know how to raise girls."

"I can't wait until this baby is born." Blythe hated being on bed rest. The next few months would be mind-numbingly boring if she had to stay in bed the whole time. After she hung up with Renie, she planned to call Lyric and see if there was anything she could be working on for RodeoChat.

"Do you need me to come back?" Renie asked.

"No, your mom needs you now. I've got plenty of people looking out for me here."

"So, how is it?"

"It's great, but something happened between Tucker and Jace."

"What?"

"He wouldn't elaborate."

"Weird."

"Yeah, that's what I think."

"When you find out, call and tell me, okay? I feel so out of it over here, on the other side of the mountains."

When they hung up, Blythe called Lyric.

"How ya doin', little mama?"

Blythe laughed. "I'm good, thanks. I'm home, well, home at my mom and dad's house. We'll be staying here for a while."

"I was gonna come and see ya later. I talked to your mom earlier. She told me you left the hospital."

"About that, I'm going to be on bed rest for a few weeks, maybe longer. I wondered if your offer to help with RodeoChat was still good."

"Of course, it is. Oh my 'lanta, I can't tell you how much I could use some help. I'm runnin' too fast, chasin' all these dreams. I can't keep 'em all straight I got so much goin' on."

"Good, because I'm going to have a lot of time on my hands."

"I can come by later, if you're not too tired. We can talk about gettin' you up and runnin'."

"That would be perfect. Hey, by the way, have you seen Bree? I've been tryin' to get in touch with her. I think her phone's off."

"Nope. How 'bout you? You seen Jace?"

"No…"

"No, what?"

"I asked Tucker about him, and he growled at me. Then he wouldn't tell me why. He's sleeping now," she whispered.

"Why'd you ask her if she'd seen me?"

"Figured it was the best way to find out what Tucker told her."

"What did she say about Bree?"

"That she hadn't been able to reach her. Said her phone was off."

"You told her you haven't seen her."

"Little white lie never hurt nothin'."

Jace shrugged.

"What was I supposed to say? That, yeah, I saw her thirty seconds before she ran out of a restaurant after seein' you with a broken nose?"

"I get your point."

"Yep, writin' a book. That's the only thing that's keepin' me sane dealin' with all of you. I got enough trouble on my hands with my own twin."

"You have a twin?"

"Yeah, and if any of you could pull your heads outta your asses long enough to pay attention to anybody else's lives, you mighta remembered that."

"There's been a lot goin' on, but yeah, I remember now. I'm sorry, Lyric."

"There's been a lot goin' on with me, too. I'm 'bout smooth out done with it all."

"Smooth out what?"

"Nothin'. It's somethin' Bullet says all the time."

"Bullet is your twin?"

"At least you catch on faster than Bree."

He doubted it, because he had no idea what Lyric was talking about. He could tell she was mad though, and he'd never seen her mad. At least he didn't think he had. Maybe he had seen her mad and wasn't paying attention.

Jace called Bree again, and for the second time, it went to voicemail. He'd left a message the first time, so he didn't leave another.

***

Bree drove straight to the cemetery at the Air Force Academy. She needed to be with Zack, to talk to him. She was so lost without him. Before he died, her life had been so full, she hadn't had time to finish school.

Now, her life had disintegrated into nothing. She had no reason to get up in the morning. She'd been telling herself that her sister needed her, but now that Tucker was back, Blythe wouldn't need her anymore.

She had left the hospital, and no one thought it was important to even let Bree know. She drove over to see her sister, and was humiliated when the nurse told her Blythe had left.

What was she even doing here? Maybe it was time to start her life over, somewhere else. She didn't know what answers she thought she'd find sitting next to Zack's grave, but she wasn't finding any.

She pulled out her phone to check the time and realized she'd turned it off earlier.

When she turned it on, there were eight messages and more texts. By the time she listened to the last one that came in, she felt stupid that she'd been feeling so sorry for herself. Her mother sounded frantic with worry.

The other message that struck her was from Jace. He called her a few minutes after she'd stormed out of the restaurant, and in his message, he told her he had to see her. There were things he needed to explain to her, and whether she believe him or not, they had nothing to do with her sister.

As much as it shouldn't be, that was the message that mattered the most to her.

Bree called her mother and told her she'd be over later, and asked her to let Blythe know she was sorry they'd missed each other.

"Are you okay?" her mother asked.

"I'm lost, Mom, trying to find my way."

"We're here if you need us, baby."

"I know. Thanks. I'll see you soon. There's another call I have to make first."

Bree ran her fingers over the lettering on Zack's tombstone as she waited for Jace to answer his phone.

***

"You're 'bout drivin' me crazy," Lyric said to Jace. She'd taken him back to the house in Palmer Lake, where he'd hoped to find Bree. She wasn't there, but Jace refused to leave until one of two things happened.

Either she came home, or she called him. Otherwise, he was staying put.

"You can leave if you want to."

"And then what? I live here, remember? Although lately, it hasn't felt much like I do."

"I'm sorry. Do your thing. Pretend I'm not here. In fact, if you want me to wait somewhere else, say the word, and I'll go wherever you point me."

"Nah, you're fine. But would you please sit down?"

Jace almost dropped his phone when it rang.

"Hi," he answered, knowing it was Bree.

"Hi." Her voice sounded remote.

"Where are you?"

"I'm with Zack. I needed somebody to talk to."

It took him a minute to figure out what she meant.

"Bree, I need to talk to you, and it's important. Can we please meet somewhere?"

"Where are you now?"

"I'm at your house."

"I can come home."

Jace looked over at Lyric, who could obviously hear what Bree was saying. She nodded her head.

"Okay. I'll wait here for you."

"Jace..."

"Yes?"

"I told you before, if you're only going to tell me that you're in love with Blythe, I already know you are, and I don't need to hear you say it."

"This has nothing to do with Blythe, except that it has something to do with Tucker. Otherwise, that's the only connection."

20

Jace was still pacing when he saw Bree's car pull into the driveway. Even though it would be the second time he told this story today, he didn't feel as though telling it again would be any easier.

He had a glass of wine waiting on the counter for her. He knew, by the time he got through his story, she'd want a glass.

"Hi," she said when she walked in the back door. She looked as though she had been crying. Now might not be the best time to tell her his story, but he didn't have a choice; he'd be gone tomorrow.

"Should we sit down?" she asked.

"Sure, if that's what you'd like to do."

She sighed. "Jace, is it what you'd like to do?"

"Uh, yeah. Let's sit."

"What did you want to tell me?"

"It's about Tucker, but it's also about me."

"Jace, I already told you—"

"It isn't about Blythe, so please, Bree, just let me talk." He could almost see the steam coming out of her ears.

She sat down on the couch in the living room, and he sat next to her.

"When Tucker and I were in high school—no it was before that, a long time before that."

She folded her arms.

"When we were in *elementary* school, we met a little girl named Rosa." He scrubbed his hand over his face, wincing when he touched his nose.

The story he continued was similar to the one Tucker told Blythe, although Jace had no way of knowing that.

"When we got into high school, Rosa and I started talking to each other more. Sometimes she'd call me after she'd been out with Tucker. At first we were just friends, but the more we talked, the more she confided in me."

Bree turned so her back was up against the arm of the couch and brought her knees up.

"Tucker wasn't exactly pressuring her into having sex with him, and the truth was, it bothered her. She thought he wasn't interested in her that way. I was quick to reassure her that he was." Jace laughed nervously.

"Go on." Bree's face was getting tighter and tighter the longer he talked. She looked as though she was giving herself a headache.

"We spent a lot of time talking about sex, which was strange at first, but then it seemed like no big deal. She had a lot of questions, and I certainly had the answers.

"In the beginning, it seemed like she wanted to be ready when Tucker was. After a while, I stopped thinking about her with Tucker—not that I ever *thought* about it, ya know—but I started thinking about her with me."

Jace took a deep breath. "One night, she suggested we meet. I don't have any idea where Tucker was, maybe hangin' with his buddies. Anyway, she asked if, instead of talking on the phone, we could talk in person. I knew it wasn't a good idea, but I did it anyway."

She asked him to pick her up at a friend's house so no one would see him or his car at her house, especially not her parents.

"She was pretty aggressive. I mean, we didn't have sex that night, but we came pretty close."

They started to make arrangements to see each other more often, and each time they did, they went a little further. When they weren't together, they talked on the phone. Rosa told him she felt as though she could talk to him in a way she'd never felt comfortable talking to Tucker.

"My ego got the best of me, that's for sure. Tuck and I competed over everything. We were always trying to outdo each other. Skiing, riding—everything. She said all the right stuff, that I excited her more than he did, that I was easier to talk to, that I understood her better than he did. I ate it up, every word.

"When we started our senior year of high school, I started pressuring her to break up with Tucker. I didn't think he was that serious about her, especially since she told me their relationship wasn't physical."

Bree got up to get another glass of wine. Jace followed and pulled another beer out for himself.

"Want something stronger?" she asked.

He wasn't sure if she was serious or being bitchy. "No thanks. Beer's good."

When she went back into the living room, he followed. He thought she might sit in one of the chairs, but she didn't. She sat back on the couch where she'd been before. This time, she covered herself with the throw that was draped over the back.

"Are you cold? Do you want me to light a fire?"

"A fire would be nice. Thanks."

"So where was I?" he asked after the fire was lit.

"Senior year."

"Yeah, anyway, I wanted her to break up with Tuck. I figured, after some time had passed, I'd tell him I was interested in her, and then she and I would start seeing each other in public."

The more Jace pressured her, the more anxious she became about it. She told him she was afraid Tucker would be angry. He kept telling her he thought she was wrong, but the truth was, she hadn't been honest about what was happening between her and Tuck.

"It got to the point where I was the one who was angry. I started asking her if she was sleeping with both me and my brother, which she insisted she wasn't.

"What she didn't tell me was that Tuck had started talking about the two of them getting married. It wasn't until I overheard Tuck talking to our dad about it, the night before Thanksgiving, that I realized how serious he was.

"I called Rosa while Tuck was still talking to my parents, and I gotta tell you, I was pissed. She kept saying she was afraid to tell him. In hindsight, I should have told him myself."

"In hindsight, maybe you shouldn't have gotten involved with your brother's girlfriend."

"In hindsight, I should become a monk or somethin'," he laughed. Bree didn't.

"Anyway, Tucker was spending Thanksgiving with her family, which was another thing I was mad as hell about."

Rosa called Jace after Tucker left their house, and told him how upset he'd been after talking with her father. She begged Jace to meet her. It hadn't been easy to come up with a reason for him to leave on

Thanksgiving, but he managed. There was a creek that ran behind her house, and they'd been meeting there when the weather was nice enough. It was warm that day, so that's where they met.

"It took her quite a while to talk down my mad. Even then, I felt as though Rosa was playin' us. I had decided to end things with her myself, and I guess she sensed it, because she started begging me not to break up with her, tellin' me how much she loved me, and all that. I was walkin' her up to the house, and she wrapped herself around me. She was kissin' me like her life depended on it when we saw somebody drive up to the house. We were far enough away that whoever it was couldn't see us, but she was quick to realize it was Tucker's truck.

"She went running up to him, begging him to listen to her. My heart was breakin', I gotta tell you. When I heard her scream for him to wait, and then got in his truck, I realized she loved him all along, and that she'd been lying to me. Maybe it was worse than that. Maybe she didn't love either one of us."

Bree was still huddled under the blanket, but her face had softened.

"Tucker told me bits and pieces about what he remembered of the accident. He also told me that she'd been trying to tell him that she was in love with someone else.

"That near broke my heart. That she'd been trying to tell him. The other thing he said was that she hadn't told him who it was before he lost control of the truck and it rolled. She was killed on impact, and Tuck was in pretty bad shape."

Jace wiped at his tears. Bree reached out from under the blanket and put her hand on his arm.

"After Tucker recovered, things got worse."

Jace told her that Tucker was hell-bent on finding who the other guy was, and that everyone believed, if he found him, he'd kill him. He'd never seen Tucker act that way, and worse, he could feel the rage inside his brother. There was sadness too—they were both feeling it—but Tucker didn't know how much of the sadness was Jace's.

"I never told anyone it was me. No one. Until today, I never told anyone any of it."

"I'm the first person you told this story?"

"No, I gotta be honest. You're not."

"Did you tell Blythe?"

"God, no. It wouldn't be my place to tell Blythe."

He told her that, when he woke up before dawn, he could feel Tucker's anguish, and that was why he got up and left. He told her about meeting up with Tucker at the scene of his accident—the one with Blythe—and how the pieces fell into place.

"Tucker realized it was me that night. That's why I look the way I do. I tried to get him to talk to me, but he wasn't havin' any part of it. I guess beatin' the shit outta me was more what he was after."

"Can you blame him?"

"No. Can't say I do."

"Now what?"

"I have no idea. I don't know what's goin' on with him and Blythe. I don't know if he'll ever want to talk to me again. I don't know nothin' about nothin'."

"And you told me because you want me to find out for you."

"No, that isn't why I told you. Jesus, Bree. You know, I already think I'm the worst guy in the world. I don't need you or anybody else makin' it worse. You think the only reason I told you this story was so you could get information for me?"

"Well, why did you tell me?"

"Fuck...I don't know. I had to, that's all I know. Somethin' inside me was sayin' that I had to be the one to tell you. 'Cause even if you don't believe me, your opinion means somethin' to me."

"Who was the other person?"

"What do you mean?"

"You said that I wasn't the first person you told this story to today. Who was?"

"Lyric."

"I see."

"What does that mean?"

"But you don't want either of us to talk to Blythe, or Tucker, right?"

"That's what we're back to; you thinkin' the worst possible thing you can about me. That I spilled my guts to you so you'd help me with my brother."

"You have to admit it's the only thing that makes sense."

"No, I don't have to admit that. Not at all. I told you because I care what you think."

"You care what Lyric thinks, too?"

"Not in the same way, no."

"Then why did you tell her?"

"Because I was scared. Okay? I've never told anyone this, Bree. No one. I carried this secret around with me for the last seven years. When Tuck was so messed up over Blythe and disappeared, I knew I had to step in and take care of her, because I owed him. I owe him everything."

"And because you love her."

"I don't know that I do. As long as I'm tellin' the truth about everything. That's the truth about Blythe. I don't know that I love her. And you wanna know why not?"

"I'm afraid to ask," she smirked.

"You think this is funny?"

"No, I'm sorry. I don't think it's funny. Go on."

"Forget it."

"No, I want to hear this. Why don't you think you're in love with my sister anymore?"

"Because of you."

"Jace, if I've led you to believe—"

"Believe that you have any feelings for me other than hatred? Nah, you haven't, Bree. You've made your feelings clear, especially in the last few minutes."

He stood.

"Where are you going? Do you want another beer?"

"No, thanks. It's time for me to go. It was important to me that I tell you my tragic story, and now that I have, there isn't any reason for me to stay."

"Wait. Listen, I'm sorry. It's a lot to take in. You can't blame me for wondering about your motives."

"That's it." Jace turned and walked out through the kitchen, slamming the back door behind him.

Blythe was running her fingers through Tucker's hair when he woke up. They were facing each other, so close she could feel his breath on her face.

"Guess I nodded off."

"You were exhausted."

"Is everything okay, Blythe?"

"Everything's okay with me, but, Tucker, I have to ask. What happened with you and Jace today?"

"It was him."

"What do you mean?"

"He was the other man. Rosa was in love with Jace."

"*No!*"

"Now you understand why I never want to hear my brother's name again."

"Oh, Tucker. I'm so sorry."

"Me, too."

"You didn't have any idea?"

"None, whatsoever. I was blindsided."

"He told you? Outright?"

"No, not exactly. We were talking about how I felt then. I told him I wasn't sure whether I ever loved Rosa. I was trying to sort through my feelings. I buried them for so long, when they came to the surface I wondered if I'd made more of it back then than it was."

"What did Jace say?"

"He said he couldn't tell. When I asked him if he remembered, he said he couldn't tell whether I loved her or not, because he couldn't differentiate his feelings from mine. That's when I figured it out. It all came together. It was him. That's why Rosa's brother said we looked alike. He was playing with me, trying to bait me. Because we did look alike, exactly alike."

"Why didn't he tell you?"

"He's a bastard, that's why. You accused me once of playing games with you. In fact, I think you accused me more than once. It was never me, darlin'. You were getting ol' Jace and me confused. He's the game player, not me. He always has been."

Blythe wanted to tell Tucker she didn't believe it. She'd never believe that it was that simple. Jace had been willing to do anything for her and the baby, and that included giving up his own chance at love. She couldn't believe the man Tucker was talking about was the same man she knew.

Tucker was hurt, and had every right to be. But he was oversimplifying what happened. If Rosa told Tucker she was in love with this other person, there had to be more to it.

"Had she told you she loved you?"

Tucker closed his eyes tightly. She wasn't sure he was going to answer. "Yes. Of course, she did."

"And were you intimate?"

"Yeah, we were."

"Do you think she and Jace—"

"I can't think about that. As it is, I never want to see him again. If I start to think about him and Rosa together, I don't think I'll be able to handle it."

Blythe gathered him close and held on tight. "I love you, Tucker."

"I know you do. And I love you. Those are the only two things I'm absolutely certain of right now. Everything else seems like a *clusterfuck* to me."

21

"I don't understand," Lyric said to Blythe.

"He left. He told Bree what happened, and then he left."

"Nobody's seen him?"

"Renie says not to worry. She's sure Billy's talked to him. They're scheduled to ride in Kansas City next weekend. Maybe he's taking a few days to get his head out of what's going on here and back into rodeo."

"What about his parents?"

No idea, Lyric. I'm telling you what I know."

Blythe thought it was odd that her friend was reacting the way she was. If anyone was a free spirit who traveled whichever way the wind blew, it was Lyric. Jace needed some time, that's all. Blythe wasn't worried about him as much as she worried about his relationship with Tucker.

"How are you feeling? Ready to work?"

"You know it. I'll go crazy doing nothing between now and when the baby's born."

"Where's Tucker?"

"Looking at houses."

"That was quick."

"I guess when you know, you know. And we know."

"Ha! Yeah, that sounds 'bout right."

"What's crazy is, my dad is with him."

"What kinda houses they lookin' at?"

"I have no idea, to tell you the truth. But Tucker is an artist, so it'll be interesting to see what appeals to him."

"Before I forget, I gotta go out of town again soon, like tomorrow."

"Business?"

"No, but I sure wish it was."

"What, then?"

"It's my brother. I've told you about him, right? Bullet?"

"You've mentioned him a couple of times. What's goin' on?"

"He's a hot mess. In a huge custody fight with his daughter's mama, got another one on the way."

"Why is she in a custody fight with him if they're having another baby?"

"The other baby isn't with her. It's with a different woman, which is what's behind the custody fight."

"Oh."

"You think things are complicated in your lives, wait 'til you hear more about mine, or my brother's. I don't have time for my life to be complicated."

"Your brother would probably think our lives are more complicated than his."

"Yeah, 'bout right, I guess. Anyway, I'm sorry to be leavin' again, but I got everything mapped out for ya."

Lyric went over a list of upcoming rodeos with Blythe who then researched websites to see who would be posting scores in real time and who wouldn't. Lyric also gave Blythe a list of contacts she could text for results at the smaller rodeos.

"You can keep your eye on Jace too this way, without him knowing about it. You'll, at least, know if he bucks off or gets a score."

It took Tucker three weeks of looking at houses daily before he found one he wanted Blythe to see. It wasn't far from Billy and Renie's ranch.

Tucker carried her to his truck, where he had pillows lined up to prop around her.

"You're going overboard."

He glared at her.

"Never mind," she laughed. "This is perfect. I'll be well-padded on every side. Will I be required to be wrapped in bunting whenever we go for a ride in your truck? Or do you think bubble wrap would work better?"

"You're on bed rest. Do you remember that part? I'm sure, if we asked the doc, he wouldn't approve a twenty-minute ride on a dirt road."

She smiled and winked at him. "I love you, Tucker Rice."

"And I love you, Blythe...Cochran."

The house was spectacular. It was under construction, but it was almost finished.

"I don't understand. Did the people building it decide they didn't want to live in it?"

"Financial issues. Anyway, it's surrounded by a little over one hundred acres, mostly forested. Isn't it great?"

"One hundred acres? I don't even know what that means."

"Well, your parents' place sits on about five acres. So we'll have twenty times more than that."

"For what? Don't tell me you want to have horses, Tucker. I'm not as into horses as Renie."

He laughed. "We don't have to have horses, Blythe, but I need space. I may add a barn at some point, but it would be more of a workshop and art studio for me than it would be to board horses."

He walked around and opened her door. "Are you ready to go inside?"

"You aren't going to carry me, are you?"

"Of course, I am." Tucker carried her up the steps and nudged the front door open with his knee. "I think this counts as carrying you over the threshold, doesn't it?"

She held up her left hand. "I don't see a ring on this hand, Mr. Rice. It doesn't count until we're officially husband and wife."

"Okay, then."

"Okay, then, what?"

"Let's look at the rest of this place."

They walked from room to room in the two-story house.

"It seems huge, Tucker."

"It's about six thousand square feet."

"Again, I don't know what that means."

"It's about the same size as your parents' house."

"But their house is ginormous. What do we need with all this space, Tucker?"

He patted her stomach. "For this little one and his brothers and sisters."

"How often do you plan to impregnate me?"

"As often as you'll let me."

Tucker led her over to the fireplace. The hearth was built up, so she could sit on it.

"What do you think?" he asked.

"I like it. But it's up to you. If you like it, that's what matters. Um…you know, can we, uh…afford it? I don't make very much money you know."

Tucker kissed her forehead. "Yes, Blythe, we can afford it."

"Tucker?"

"Yeah?"

"What about your house in Spain? And your condo in Aspen, the one you share with Jace?"

Tucker didn't want to talk about the condo, but he was going to have to get used to talking to Blythe about everything. Not only the easy stuff, the hard stuff, too.

"I signed the condo over to Jace. He owns it outright now."

"Does that mean you've talked to him?"

No, it didn't, he told her. He'd asked his father to handle it through their family's attorney. Since they were brothers, a simple quitclaim deed took care of it. As far as the place in Spain, they didn't need to worry about it for now. He wanted to take her and the baby there when they could travel. After that, they'd decide what to do about it together.

"Tucker?"

"You're full of questions today, aren't you?"

"We're making a lot of assumptions. Just because we're having a baby together doesn't mean we automatically have to start making all these decisions. Maybe we should figure out, you know, if we're going to be together, or not, first."

He knelt down in front of her and pulled her in, close to him. "You like it when I make decisions for you," he winked.

"I do, when you're picking restaurants, or what we're going to eat, but when it's about the rest of our lives, maybe you should let me give you my opinion."

"Okay, then," he reached into his pocket. "What is your opinion of this ring? It's the one I picked out in order to ask you to marry me."

Blythe stared down at the ring he had in his hand. It was an emerald-cut diamond, flanked by two similar-sized emeralds. "It's magnificent," she said.

"Since you think so," he slipped it on her finger. "Would you like to give me your opinion about marrying me?"

"I would love to marry you." She kissed him. "I love you, Tucker."

"I love you, Blythe. So, what do you think of the house?"

"Also magnificent, even if it is a bit big."

"So it's a yes to the ring, a yes to marriage, and a yes to the house?"

"Yes, to all of the above."

She and Tucker walked through the house a couple more times and talked about which room they would use as a nursery, and what they might do with the others. When Blythe yawned Tucker told her it was time for him to get her back to her parents' house. "Your dad is preparing a celebration feast."

"Why?"

"Bree is coming over, and I heard a rumor that Liv and Ben are in town with little Caden, which means we are expecting Billy, Renie, and Willow, too. Oh, and Dottie and Bill. And Lyric. I think that about covers it."

Someone was missing. They both knew it—it didn't need to be said. It had been over a month since anyone had heard from Jace. Tucker told Blythe that his mother said he was okay; that he was taking time for himself. When his mom asked if he wanted to know where Jace was, or how to get in touch with him, Tucker declined.

"You're both my children, and I hate to see you and Jace at odds. He's your brother, Tucker," she reminded him.

It wasn't a reminder he needed.

* * *

On October 3, Cochran Henry Rice was born at two in the morning. Bree was in the delivery room with Blythe and Tucker, for moral support.

She pulled out her phone and took photos of the baby boy as he was weighed and measured, and then wrapped in a blanket and handed to his mother. She took another picture of Tucker kissing first Cochran then Blythe.

She texted every one of them to the same number she'd texted periodically over the last few months. She never got a response, so she didn't know whether it was still Jace's number. If it was, she wanted him to see the first photos of their nephew—Aunt Bree and Uncle Jace. He told her once, that they better figure out how to get along because he knew they both planned to be a part of this baby's life.

EPILOGUE

It had been four months since Jace left Monument. Instead of heading to Crested Butte as everyone expected him to, he went north.

He'd called Billy the day after he left Colorado. He owed him and Irene that much. They'd been good to him; he considered both of them friends.

"Take the time you need," Billy had told him "There ain't nobody I know who hasn't done somethin' they regret, Jace, especially when they were a teenager. You don't wanna hear my stories. I got a hella lot of 'em."

He thanked Billy and told him he'd be in touch. He had no idea when, but when he was ready, he would be.

"You come see us whenever you want. You're always welcome here," Irene told him when Billy handed her the phone.

In the weeks that followed, Jace competed in more regional rodeos than he could remember. After the first couple, they all started blending together. Each morning when he woke up, it took him a while to figure out where the hell he was. Once he did, he had to figure out where the hell he was going next. He traveled around

Montana and Idaho, and then he traveled to Wyoming to compete in Cheyenne.

Now he was somewhere in Montana, he wasn't sure where. He'd been driving all night, headed to a stock contractor's place. Someone at the last rodeo he was at told him there was an outfit up north, looking for help.

His phone pinged, and he knew who the text was from. Bree was the only one he ever heard from, other than his mother, who didn't text—she called.

He didn't hear from her often, but this time, he'd been expecting it. He pulled off on the side of the road and looked at the pictures she'd sent. His eyes filled with tears as he scrolled through the photos of his newborn nephew. Her last text said, *Cochran Henry Rice, born 2:10 AM, nine pounds, four ounces, twenty-one inches.*

He'd never wished he could be in two places at once more than he did right now. If only there was a way he could get back to Colorado to see his nephew, and his brother. But he couldn't, mainly because he wouldn't be welcome.

Tucker knew how to reach him if he wanted to, and he hadn't. He could feel it, or better put, he couldn't feel it. Tucker was completely shut off from him. He had been for months.

If he was being honest with himself—and these days, he was trying damn hard to be—he'd have to admit he'd been hiding out most of the last seven years. That's what working at the dude ranch in Colorado had been all about.

No one knew him there. They didn't know his background; they didn't know his brother. When he was there, he was Jace Rice, an easy-going cowboy. He flirted with the guests, who soaked it in, and then left when their six-day vacation was over.

Until the day Irene Fairchild set foot on the ranch, he hadn't been interested in getting to know anyone well enough that their lives would cross again after the summer ended. She had changed everything.

In less than a year, he'd gone from that carefree cowboy to one who had to face the pain he'd worked hard to bury. In doing so, he lost his brother. It made him sick to his stomach whenever he thought about it.

It would be easy to blame Tucker, say he was being an asshole about it. Billy was right, who didn't fuck up when they were a teenager? Everyone did. Even Tucker had. But he couldn't blame his brother. He'd had every chance in the world to come clean.

Of his many regrets, he didn't know which one was the biggest. Getting involved with Rosa? That had started the chain of events that had come to a crashing conclusion four months ago.

He also regretted the way things had ended with Bree. It had been important to him to be the one to tell her the story himself, and when she'd questioned his motives, he got angry.

The fact that she texted meant a lot to him. There had been several times he wanted to pick up the phone and call her. Or at the very least, text her back. But why? Her sister was married to his brother—the brother who never wanted to see him again. As much as he'd been drawn to Bree, leaving then had been best. She had plenty of her own shit to work through.

He never answered, because he wanted her to forget about him. He wanted to forget himself. How ironic was it that only a few months ago, Tucker had wanted the same thing? He ran after the accident, intending to leave his previous life behind. Now Jace was the one who'd left his life.

He pulled into a diner in Helena around dawn. He'd get something to eat here, find a place to stay, and then head out in search of the Beiman Rough Stock Company.

The Beimans were big in Alberta, Canada, and old man Beiman had been inducted into the Pro Rodeo Hall of Fame in the early nineties. Jace remembered hearing about the rough stock contractor's death a few years ago. He'd died in a car accident along with another rancher known for breaking horses and raising cattle. The loss of both men had been a tragedy talked about often in the rodeo world.

Beiman's sons had taken over the rough stock business, but it was becoming too much for the family. Jace heard that they were looking for help in the way of contractors, but he also heard they were looking for a partner, someone to take over the Montana operation.

If what he'd heard was true, he planned to make the ranch outside Helena, Montana, his new home—at least for the time being. He didn't allow himself to think too far ahead. Whenever he did, he couldn't stand the loneliness he predicted would define the rest of his life.

The meeting with the Beimans lasted a little over two hours. As it turned out, they weren't looking for a partner as much as they were looking to sell. If he did this, it would mean tying up almost all of his money in the ranch. It wasn't a decision he wanted to make without talking it over with his parents. He called his father, who agreed to fly up the next day.

Jace almost cried when he hung up. He missed his family; he hadn't realized how much. He wished he could talk to Tuck about it, too. This was the kind of thing his brother would have loved to see Jace do. He would have helped Jace come up with a name for the ranch and would have wanted to design a new brand. Jace couldn't imagine that he'd ever like anything any-one but his brother designed.

His mother came along, and his parents stayed in Helena for two weeks. When they left, his parents were his partners in a 12,000-acre business venture they named Triple-Bar-R Rough Stock and Cattle Company.

It hadn't worked out the way Jace had originally planned, but his father was unrelenting in his insistence that he wanted to be a partner in his son's venture. Jace only had to liquidate half of his holdings to make the deal; both his parents put up the rest of the capital needed. They were headed back to Aspen now but intended to come back and settle in one of the two main houses already built on the ranch property.

For the second time in as many weeks, Jace found himself on the verge of tears. Having his parents close was something he hadn't even considered. Maybe the on-going ache of loneliness would be somewhat dimin-ished by knowing they were within arms' reach.

* * *

The day Bree graduated with her master's degree was bittersweet. Her whole family was there, even Brooke and her husband flew in from Germany. No matter how many people surrounded her, it didn't make up for the two who didn't. Everyone knew she'd be missing Zack today, but no one knew there was someone else she wished was there.

It had been almost a year, but she still thought about Jace almost every day, especially when she was with Cochran. When she wasn't studying or working on her thesis, Bree spent as much time as she could with Blythe and the baby.

She helped them furnish and decorate the house in Black Forest, and offered to babysit at least once a week, so Blythe and Tucker could have some time alone. They usually went out for dinner, which meant they were gone less than two hours, but Bree lived for that time with her nephew.

He was growing up so fast, and Jace was missing it. She took pictures and wanted to text them to him, but since he never responded when she did, she wondered if maybe he didn't want to see them. So she eventually stopped.

After the graduation ceremony, they went back to her parents' house, where they were hosting a barbecue. She spent most of the afternoon waging a battle with threatening tears.

Blythe asked her if she wanted to go for a walk with her and Cochran.

"I could tell you were uncomfortable," Blythe told her.

"Emotional more than uncomfortable."

"You miss him."

"Zack? Of course, I do. I miss him every day." The tears she fought hard to keep control of began to fall. Thinking about Zack made her think of Jace. How crazy was that? But he would've understood how she was feeling today, if no one else did. God, she missed him.

"Not Zack, Bree. I know you miss Jace."

That made her cry harder. "I do. I miss him so much. Is that horrible, Blythe? Am I a terrible person? I miss Jace more than I miss Zack."

"I don't think that's true. I think you miss both of them. They're intertwined. Jace became someone you leaned on after Zack died."

"Jace was…a friend, I suppose. I didn't even know him very well. It's silly that I miss him. Has Tucker talked to him?"

"No, but we talk to his parents. They moved to Montana. Jace bought a ranch and they're going to help him run it."

"Jace bought a ranch? Why?"

"I'm not sure, but Hank and Carol are partners with him in it."

"Where is it?"

"Somewhere near Helena, I think. I'll call his mom this week and see what else I can find out. When I do, I'll let you know."

"He's raising rough stock," Blythe told her a few days later when Bree was having lunch with her and Lyric.

"What's that?"

"What's what?" asked Lyric.

"Rough stock," answered Bree.

"You know, broncs and bulls."

"Rodeo broncs and bulls?"

"Well, yeah," Lyric rolled her eyes. "What else would someone raise them for?"

"Does he know what he's doing?"

"He must. It's a big investment. I wouldn't think he'd get into it if he didn't."

Bree wanted to change the subject. She thought about Jace Rice too much as it was. Imagining him working a ranch in Montana wasn't helping. Picturing him on the back of a horse, his face weathered from days spent riding...she fanned herself.

"Have you decided what you're going to do next?"

"I've been applying for teaching positions. I may have a chance at a temporary position at the Air Force Academy. It's at the junior faculty level, and only for two years, but it's a start."

"You aren't moving out?"

"I hadn't planned on it, but I suppose I could find another place if you needed me to."

"No, not at all. I thought you might be leaving the area."

"Why would she be leaving the area?" Blythe asked Lyric.

"Relax, Blythe. It's all good. I'm hardly ever home anyway. I thought you'd have to get a job out of state or somethin'."

"I have a babysitting position I'm not willing to let go of," she smiled. "I love that little boy so much," Bree murmured.

"And he loves you." Blythe reached over and rubbed Bree's shoulder. "He'd miss his Auntie Bree, so you better not be thinking of moving away."

"Okay, I'll fess up. I had another reason for askin'."

Oh God, what was Lyric about to say?

"It's my brother; he's havin' a pretty hard time of it. I need to get him out of Oklahoma. And it isn't only him. He's got a wife and new baby. They need a fresh start, and I was hopin' it could be here."

"Oh."

"Don't worry about it, Bree. I'll figure somethin' out. Maybe find a little house for them to rent."

"Who's working the boarding stables at Billy and Renie's place?" Blythe asked. "Your brother knows horses, doesn't he? Maybe he could work for them."

Blythe picked up her phone as though she was going to make a call, and then set it back down again.

"You know, there's a small house on the edge of the property, between our place and Patterson Ranch, that no one has lived in for a couple of years. Maybe the Pattersons would consider letting your brother stay there in exchange for workin' the ranch."

"How do you know all this?" Bree asked.

"We see Dottie and Bill all the time now that we live next door. Dottie has been teaching me how to cook."

Bree shook her head. There were days she hardly recognized her baby sister.

Lyric looked at Bree again, as though she expected her to say something.

"What?"

"I don't know, you seem restless."

"I do?"

"You're in a rut."

She was? Maybe Lyric was right.

"I have two months before I start teaching, if I get the position at the academy that is. I should know this week. It might be a good time for me to travel."

"There you go," Lyric smiled. "Where?"

"It's been a long time since I've gone fishing."

"Fishing?"

"You don't know this, but Bree is a master fly-fisherwoman," Blythe told Lyric.

"A what?"

"Fly-fishing. I love it."

"And she's good at it," Blythe added.

"Why?" Lyric asked, not seeming to understand at all.

"It's very relaxing, but challenging at the same time. I like the solitude of it."

Now that she thought about it, it would be exactly what she needed. Time alone to get her head back on straight.

She needed to grieve her husband and stop thinking about Jace Rice. He'd become a crutch. If she thought about him, she didn't have to think about the pain of losing Zack. If she was honest with herself—and she was trying to be—she had to recognize it for what it was.

She had to force herself to work through the stages of grief she was trying hard to avoid. She knew the time had come for her to face it.

Ten days later, Bree left for Stanley, Idaho. She would be spending the next four weeks at Idaho Rocky Mountain Ranch. She'd fish, and ride...and mourn. When she came back, she'd spend every day teaching cadets, ones just like her husband had been.

What had she gotten herself into?

About the Author

USA Today and Amazon Top 15 Bestselling Author Heather Slade writes shamelessly sexy, edge-of-your seat romantic suspense.

She gave herself the gift of writing a book for her own birthday one year. Forty-plus books later (and counting), she's having the time of her life.

The women Slade writes are self-confident, strong, with wills of their own, and hearts as big as the Colorado sky. The men are sublimely sexy, seductive alphas who rise to the challenge of capturing the sweet soul of a woman whose heart they'll hold in the palm of their hand forever. Add in a couple of neck-snapping twists and turns, a page-turning mystery, and a swoon-worthy HEA, and you'll be holding one of her books in your hands.

She loves to hear from my readers. You can contact her at heather@heatherslade.com

To keep up with her latest news and releases, please visit her website at www.heatherslade.com to sign up for her newsletter.

MORE FROM AUTHOR HEATHER SLADE

BUTLER RANCH
Kade's Worth
Brodie's Promise
Maddox's Truce
Naughton's Secret
Mercer's Vow
Kade's Return
Butler Ranch Christmas

WICKED WINEMAKERS FIRST LABEL
Brix's Bid
Ridge's Release
Press' Passion
Zin's Sins
Tryst's Temptation

WICKED WINEMAKERS SECOND LABEL
Beau's Beloved
Coming Soon:
Cru's Crush
Bones' Bliss
Snapper's Seduction
Kick's Kiss

ROARING FORK RANCH
Coming Soon:
Roaring Fork Wrangler
Roaring Fork Roughstock
Roaring Fork Rockstar
Roaring Fork Rooker
Roaring Fork Bridger

THE ROYAL AGENTS OF MI6
Make Me Shiver
Drive Me Wilder
Feel My Pinch
Chase My Shadow
Find My Angel

K19 SECURITY SOLUTIONS TEAM ONE
Razor's Edge
Gunner's Redemption
Mistletoe's Magic
Mantis' Desire
Dutch's Salvation

K19 SECURITY SOLUTIONS TEAM TWO
Striker's Choice
Monk's Fire
Halo's Oath
Tackle's Honor
Onyx's Awakening

K19 SHADOW OPERATIONS TEAM ONE
Code Name: Ranger
Code Name: Diesel
Code Name: Wasp
Code Name: Cowboy
Code Name: Mayhem

K19 ALLIED INTELLIGENCE TEAM ONE
Code Name: Ares
Code Name: Cayman
Code Name: Poseidon
Code Name: Zeppelin
Code Name: Magnet

K19 ALLIED INTELLIGENCE TEAM TWO
Coming Soon:
Code Name: Puck
Code Name: Michelangelo
Code Name: Typhon
Code Name: Hornet
Code Name: Reaper

PROTECTORS UNDERCOVER
Undercover Agent
Undercover Emissary
Coming Soon:
Undercover Savior
Undercover Infidel
Undercover Assassin

THE INVINCIBLES TEAM ONE
Decked
Edged
Grinded
Riled
Smoked

THE INVINCIBLES TEAM TWO
Bucked
Irished
Sainted
Hammered
Ripped

THE UNSTOPPABLES TEAM ONE
Furied
Merried

COWBOYS OF CRESTED BUTTE
A Cowboy Falls
A Cowboy's Dance
A Cowboy's Kiss
A Cowboy Stays
A Cowboy Wins